A MAN CALLED BLUE

Blue wound up in Fall Creek, looking for work. Instead, he found trouble in the form of a cowboy seeking to make his name as a gunfighter. But the man was no match for Blue and soon paid the ultimate price. Having demonstrated his skills so dramatically, Blue was hired as foreman for the ST Ranch owned by a young woman, Ellen Turner. Then a land baron, unable to buy the ranch from Ellen, burned it down and confiscated the property. But he hadn't reckoned on the dogged perseverance of Blue and his friend, Noah . . .

Books by Paul K. McAfee in the Linford Western Library:

BONNER
THE DARK TRAIL
CABEL
BEYOND THE BLUE MESA

SPECIAL MESSAGE TO READERS

This book is published under the auspices of

THE ULVERSCROFT FOUNDATION

(registered charity No. 264873 UK)

Established in 1972 to provide funds for research, diagnosis and treatment of eye diseases. Examples of contributions made are: —

A Children's Assessment Unit at Moorfield's Hospital, London.

•

Twin operating theatres at the Western Ophthalmic Hospital, London.

•

A Chair of Ophthalmology at the Royal Australian College of Ophthalmologists.

•

The Ulverscroft Children's Eye Unit at the Great Ormond Street Hospital For Sick Children, London.

You can help further the work of the Foundation by making a donation or leaving a legacy. Every contribution, no matter how small, is received with gratitude. Please write for details to:

THE ULVERSCROFT FOUNDATION,
The Green, Bradgate Road, Anstey,
Leicester LE7 7FU, England.
Telephone: (0116) 236 4325

In Australia write to:

THE ULVERSCROFT FOUNDATION,
c/o The Royal Australian College of Ophthalmologists,
27, Commonwealth Street, Sydney, N.S.W. 2010.

PAUL K. McAFEE

A MAN CALLED BLUE

Complete and Unabridged

LINFORD
Leicester

First published in Great Britain in 2001 by
Robert Hale Limited
London

First Linford Edition
published 2002
by arrangement with
Robert Hale Limited
London

British Library CIP Data

McAfee, Paul K.
A man called Blue.—Large print ed.—
Linford western library
1. Western stories
2. Large type books
I. Title
823.9′14 [F]

ISBN 0–7089–9946–8

Published by
F. A. Thorpe (Publishing)
Anstey, Leicestershire

Set by Words & Graphics Ltd.
Anstey, Leicestershire
Printed and bound in Great Britain by
T. J. International Ltd., Padstow, Cornwall

This book is printed on acid-free paper

This book is dedicated with deep love, to my wife Shirley, whose love and support keeps me writing and in appreciation of George, David, Ronald and Mark

1

He came into Fall Creek as the sun was touching the peaks of the mountains which surrounded the town. He reined in his black horse at the beginning of a street, leading through a cluster of buildings which formed the center of the town. At least three smaller streets, or alleys, led off to the right and left, each corner taken by a saloon, an eatery, and at the far end of the street a sign which informed the traveler that there was a marshal's office and a jail.

He grimaced and sat relaxed in the saddle; a tall, taciturn man, wearing a worn, dark hat, the brim now pulled low against the glint of the setting sun. His face was tanned from years of sun and wind of many places west of the big river. Clad in dark blue pants, worn and faded. His boots were of good leather, but in need of polishing and care.

About his slim waist was a belt studded with the brass shells of ammunition for his Colt .44, which was thrust into a holster, a small leather loop over the hammer, to prevent discharge in case of a hard run, or being thrown by something exciting the horse. He was an excellent rider, and had conquered many a spell of bucking by half-broken cayuses. This horse, a beautiful black stallion, pawed impatiently at the ground, flickering his ears as though in protest of this sudden inactivity.

The butt of the Colt was worn. There were no notches marring its smooth surface. But it was worn, settled in place, as though part of his body. Back of the saddle was his roll of blankets, groundsheet and other personal items, including a smaller, .41 caliber pistol, as a spare.

All in all, he presented the figure of a man at home on his horse, carrying with him the 'possibles' needed for whatever occasion confronted him. His face, angular and at the moment beard-darkened, was highlighted by grey-green Scottish eyes, which could squint in a sudden laughter or tighten and send glints of anger as a situation might call for. At the moment he narrowed his vision allowing him to see through the glare of the setting sun, taking in the sight of the town's main street before him.

Finally, straightening in the saddle he gigged his horse gently in the flanks, and guided it down the street, drawing up before the marshal's office. He dismounted, stretched tiredly, and looping the reins over a hitch rail, stepped up on the boardwalk before the lawman's office and looked at the door. It was locked. Across one corner of the door was a spider-web holding two or three captured insects. He studied the scene briefly and turning about, looked up the street toward the nearest saloon. Two or three horses stood slack-hipped before the hitch rail, tails switching now and then against some irritation.

Taking the reins in his left hand, his

right hand swinging close to the butt of his pistol, he strolled up the street and added his horse to those standing before the saloon. He looped the reins over the rail and once again mounted the boardwalk. Batwing doors opened into a large room. Over the top of the doors he could see a bar which stretched the length of the room. Tables and chairs sat about, one table being occupied by three men playing a slow game of five-card stud. He pushed the doors open and stepped through. Pausing momentarily he stood, letting his gaze adjust to the dimness of the room, and taking in the light activity. He pushed back his hat and walked to the bar.

The barman moved up the length of the pine surface, swiping with a damp rag at a few spots, and stood before him.

'What'll it be? Whiskey or beer?'

The man eyed the barkeep, noting the protruding belly, attesting to the man's frequent tippling of his own stock.

'A beer.'

'Outta beer. Just whiskey.'

He eyed the barkeep quizzically. 'Then why did you offer beer or whiskey?'

The man shrugged and grinned. 'Just makin' conversation, I guess.' The barkeep eyed him closely, noting the sixgun slung low on the right hip. Leather strings to tie it down tightly to the leg dangled below the holster.

'My name's Higgens,' he continued. 'Care to give me your moniker?'

The barkeep was eyed steadily by grey-green Scots eyes, the face expressionless. Then, taking a sip from the whiskey and clearing his throat, the man answered softly.

'Just call me 'Blue'. That's what I'm usually called, whenever it's necessary to give it.'

One of the card-players lifted his head, eyeing the man at the bar. Tossing his cards into the center of the table, he pushed back his chair and rose.

'Did you say your moniker is Blue?'

Blue turned slowly, his whiskey glass in his left hand, his right hand resting lightly on the edge of the bar. He eyed the questioner slowly, taking in the range clothes, the sixgun on the right hip, the slightly straddled stance. This man is pining for a gun play, he mused. And I came here to get away from just such happenings. He nodded.

'Yes. Why?'

The man stepped away from the table, squaring with Blue, his eyes narrowing. 'I heard of a fellow called 'Blue' that was a gun-slick and mixed up in the sheep and cattle war down in the Arizona rim-rock country. Might that be you?'

Blue looked at him steadily. He lifted the whiskey to his lips and finished his drink, placing the glass on the bar.

'You are inquisitive, friend,' he said. 'Most of us on this side of the big river have moved around a bunch. But that gives anyone the right to answer such questions if he wants to. I don't think I care to tell you the story of my life.'

'Then you're ashamed of what you did there? I heard that a bunch of gun-slicks did a lot of killin' just because they had the chance to show off their way with a pistol.'

Blue shrugged.

The man stepped further away from the table and looked at Blue with narrowed gaze. His jaw muscles twisted and his right hand spread, the fingers quivering over the butt of his gun.

'Just stop right there, Eli. I ain't gonna have no gun-play in my saloon. So ease up on that strong talk. If you have a crow to pick with this pilgrim, take it outside.' The barkeep leveled a long-barreled Greener shotgun over the bar, and the click of his earing back the hammers echoed through the room.

'Aw, Higgens,' Eli said, 'you pull that Greener of yours every time someone moves.' He sneered at Blue. 'Come on outside an' we'll see who will come out best.'

Blue shook his head. 'I came in for a drink and a little bit of information, not a gunfight. Besides, the minute the guns began the marshal would be on us, badge and all, and toss us into the slammer.'

'Coward, huh? Just as I thought. Let a good man brace 'em and most gunnies will back down.

'Come on out in the street. We ain't got no marshal in town. So you don't have to worry about that. Besides, when this fracas is over, you won't have anything to worry about.' Eli sneered at Blue and turning, swaggered out of the saloon, leaving the batwing doors swinging behind him.

The men playing cards with Eli looked at the stranger and suddenly knew that here was something they did not want to become involved in. This man's eyes showed purpose, his face remained expressionless except for a small muscle that worked in the flesh of a cheek.

He eyed the two men at the table and, turning to the bar, slowly unbuckled his gunbelt and laid it before Higgens.

'I'll be back in a few minutes for this.'

'You goin' out there unarmed? Why, that Eli won't care about you not packin' iron. He's bad, an' any notch on his gun-butt is a chance for him to brag a little more. Keep your pistol ready an' watch out, he's tricky.'

Blue shook his head. 'This is the way I'll meet him.' And he turned away and walked to the door, opening the batwing doors and stepping through.

As he did so, he raised his arms. Eli stood in the street watching and waiting and when Blue appeared, unarmed, and with his hands raised to his shoulders, he was startled and his hand, already darting toward his holster, paused in midair.

'Where's your pistol? You really are a coward, ain't you.'

Blue stood on the boardwalk staring at him.

'Nope. I'm no coward. But I'm in no mood for a gunfight. Just shuck your belt and iron, and we'll settle our differences, which is entirely your own, without pistols.'

Eli stared at him and then leered. 'Right. I don't need no gun to settle your hash.' He unbuckled his gunbelt and handed it to one of the men he had played cards with. 'Here, hold this. It won't take me long.'

Blue stepped off the boardwalk into the street, his arms by his side, his body seemingly relaxed. Eli approached and circled about him, his fists up and moving in what he believed to be boxer style, or so the penny magazines from Chicago and St Louis sported. He grinned as Blue made no move, but simply turned with him, watching his every motion.

Suddenly Eli yelled and dived headlong at Blue, intending to butt him in the stomach and then pommel him fist and foot, street-brawling style. Blue was watching and as Eli rushed, he stepped aside and as the man brushed past him, twisted and drove a hard fist into Eli's kidney area. Eli yelled and skidded to a halt, his lunge misfiring. He straightened and eyed Blue carefully.

The fist in the kidneys was unexpected. He had visions of Blue capitulating after the first rush. But here his opponent stood, cool, with no expression.

Eli charged again, with fists fanning, his body turning and twisting, attempting to break through the barrier of Blue's sinewy arms and shoulders. He landed some fierce blows on Blue, who rode out the rain of his attack, and then, settling on his heels, drove rights and lefts into the body and face of his opponent.

Suddenly, seeing that it was evident Eli was losing the fight, one of his companions from the poker-table tensed. As Blue backed up close to him, to the circle of onlookers, he stuck out a foot and tripped him. As Blue staggered backwards, Eli bored in and slammed a fist into his midriff, and then a wild looping right to the chin. Blue saw stars and staggered away toward the center of the ring gathered about them. He was tiring, but was in no panic. Eli, following him, grinned in triumph. He had his man! Drawing back for another wide, swinging right he opened himself to Blue, and met a right to the face, smashing his nose, and a heavy left fist burying itself in his stomach. He yelled and bent over, struggling for breath, and met the smash of Blue's knee to his chin. His teeth clicked together and he fell over in the dust of the street, stunned and bleeding from the mouth and nose.

Watching Eli push himself to his feet, Blue saw the man's hand drop to his boot top, appearing with a slender bladed knife. Holding it, blade upward, in a knife-fighter's stance, Eli couched and moved toward Blue, his narrow face bloodied, his eyes glaring insanely. Blue backed away from him.

'This was to be a fist-fight,' Blue said, his eyes watching the movement of the knife as they would the poised fangs of a snake. 'I'm clean, and I expected you to be the same. Put the pig-sticker down and we'll finish this fracas man to man.'

Eli shook his head. 'I'm gonna cut you from eyeballs to belly,' he yelled. 'No man beats me in a fight, guns, fists or knives. Now, get yourself ready, for you're about to meet your Maker!'

He dived in toward Blue, his knife-hand slashing back and up, directing the blade toward Blue's middle. Blue quickly grasped his wrist, and turning, twisted the arm, feeling tendons snap. He heard Eli yelling in pain. The knife dropped to the ground and Blue pushed the man away. As Eli straightened, Blue stepped in with a whipping left into the side, and as the man gasped and fell back, a hard right to the temple. Eli staggered, his eyes rolling back in his head, and fell over his knife, unconscious.

Blue turned to the circle about him, cold eyes looking for the one who had tripped him, but Eli's friends had disappeared when they saw their buddy lose the knife, and then fall, out cold.

Seeing the men were gone, Blue walked tiredly to a horse-trough nearby and splashed water on his face and head. Sitting on the edge of the boardwalk, he wiped his face with his bandanna and looked up as Higgens, the bartender, leaned over him.

'Stranger, are you able to walk? If so, come on in an' the drink's on me. An' you can get your hardware.'

Blue struggled to his feet. 'Sounds about right to me, friend. And I'm called Blue.' He followed the barkeep into the saloon and leaning against the bar, sipped the whiskey slowly. It bit at the bruised places in his mouth and he winced at the sting.

'Where're you headed, Blue?' Higgens asked.

Blue shrugged. 'I was just riding through, and thought I'd ask about work hereabouts.'

Higgens shook his head. 'There's not much doin' around here, Blue. You might stick around a few days, however. Roundup's a few weeks away an' someone might be needin' a hand.'

The batwing door swung open and a heavy-set man, tugging at his wide-brimmed hat, ambled to the bar. Heavy-faced, with red lines tracing through his cheeks and nose informed anyone who looked closely that here was one who indulged in good liquor frequently. Apparently he must have a source of such liquid himself, for the saloon certainly did not offer much over the bar. This ran through Blue's mind as he eyed the man carefully. So far as he could see the man was unarmed.

He came to the bar beside Blue and wiggled a finger at Higgens.

'Pour me a jigger of your best, which, I am aware, is also your worst, distilled in your kitchen about a day ago.'

'Now, Mayor. Don't go runnin' down my stock, 'specially before the stranger here. He might get to thinkin' your way an' not order any more.'

The rotund man looked at Blue and raised his glass. 'Here's to you, stranger.

You did a right good job on that bully, Eli Whitted. He's always looking for a fight and this time he found more than he bargained for.'

'I'm not a trouble hunter. But I draw the line now and then and defend it.'

The man nodded, placed his emptied glass on the bar and held out a hand to Blue.

'I'm Homer Ragsdale, the chairman of the town council. Maybe Higgens told you we have no marshal at the present.'

Blue nodded. 'I heard,' he said. 'From what I just went through, and a complete stranger in the town, seems like you need a marshal to keep down street brawls, to say the least.'

Ragsdale looked at him thoughtfully. 'You handled yourself very well out there. Have you ever done any law work? Marshal, sheriff in some part of the country?'

Blue shook his head. 'No. Not that I'm shy of the law. I've got a clean slate. You'll find no flyers with my picture on them. But, no, I've never done any kind of work like that.'

Ragsdale eyed him unwaveringly. 'Then how would you like to be marshal of Fall Creek?'

2

Ellen Turner looked out over the meadow below her cabin and counted the pure-bred Herefords grazing there. Her bull, huge and beautiful in the sun, grazed in another fenced field close to the barn and sheds. Her father had started this herd, breeding for weight and firm flesh, and had made one shipment East to factories crying out for more and more beef. Almost immediately there had come requests for her animals, in particular veal.

Now, the herd was small. Somehow, someone had rustled a dozen or so of her prime cattle. The seed bull was kept in the small pasture close to the barns and had not been stolen. Bitterly, she thought of the future.

Just when it looked as if her father's long seasons in breeding the animals he wanted had brought him to the edge of success, he was found dead in a back pasture, and a small herd of his regular breed of cattle were gone. Tracks led into the mountains, and disappeared.

Silas Turner had come into the Dakotas immediately following the Civil War. A veteran of many battles from Shiloh to Savannah, Georgia, he had homesteaded the amount of acreage allowed, and with free-range grazing rights, had decided on producing cattle which would, in the long run, bring him better income and need less work in care than the regular cattle, range-bred and somewhat wild.

It was on a late autumn day that he had been in the back pasture checking on the small herd of Herefords. No one heard the shot fired. The small hills about the pasture echoed briefly with the sound of the long-range rifle that had sped a bullet through his back, tearing out his heart on its passage through his body. He was not found for three days, when Mel Lewis, foreman of the ST brand, went searching at the daughter's request.

Now he rested in the small family cemetery on the crest of a small knoll back of the house among some aspens. He was beside his wife, who had died in child-birth when their daughter, Ellen, was six years old. He had reared the girl, training her as he would have the son that died at birth. She could ride, rope and do well many of those things on a ranch that the owner's daughter would never be expected otherwise to do. She carried on the breeding and development of the special brand begun by her father.

Just when it seemed she was winning the battle against the elements, the scorns of neighboring ranchers at her large cattle, just when she was planning to increase her herd, someone was rustling her stock.

A loan was due at the bank, taken to purchase special food for the cattle.

It was time to go see Homer Ragsdale at the Fall Creek bank. Her dad had used the banking facilities ever since they had come here. The old owner, Silas Turner's friend and fellow poker-player, had died and a nephew, Homer Ragsdale, was now the bank president. Ellen had never met him nor done any business with him. She only knew him by sight and that he was also the chairman of the town council.

She walked over to the tack shed where Hoppy Jackson, the ranch cook and handyman, was working on a set of harness. He looked up as she approached.

'Hoppy, is Mel Lewis around?' Now that her father was dead, she had to depend largely upon the foreman.

'Nope, Miss Ellen. He went to the back pastures where your daddy was — where he was found. Thought he might find some tracks that would tell him something.'

'I'm going into town, Hoppy. Would you saddle the mare for me?'

Hoppy had been mauled by a wild stallion on a horse-hunt a few years back. One leg was badly broken and twisted. Consequently he walked with a dragging limp, with a little hop when he rose from wherever he was seated. He laid down the harness and got off the stool he was sitting on.

'Sure thing, Miss Ellen. Have her ready for you in a jiffy.' He grinned a rather toothless grin.

Ellen returned to the house and busied herself getting ready for the trip. She was in her mid-twenties, in the blooming years of her womanhood. With dark-blue eyes, dark hair and clear complexion, her face portrayed a straightforwardness that caught the interest of those she met. Her smile was radiant, showing white, well-cared-for teeth, which was rare in this country populated chiefly by males and without the benefits of the East's modern dental care with doctors and dentists for guidance.

She was athletic and when Hoppy brought her mare to her, she mounted with a lithe movement, seating firmly in the saddle, showing familiarity with horses. Her direct, honest gaze, her smile, readily given, and her obvious womanhood, an attractive body, full bosom and slim waist, brought her many proposals. None of which, to date, she had accepted.

'You be careful with your talk with Homer Ragsdale, Miss Ellen,' the elderly former cowboy advised, handing the reins to her. 'He's a slick one. An' he wouldn't hesitate a minute on flim-flammin' you somewhere along the line.'

She accepted the reins and smiled at him. 'I know Homer pretty well, Hoppy. I don't think he can pull any wool over my eyes.'

She gigged the mare in the flanks and trotted out of the barn-yard. Briefly she wondered why the foreman, Mel Lewis, was still looking for tracks. It had been six months since her father had been murdered. Weather had obliterated tracks, grass had grown where the body had lain, and any signs left by the shooter, would have vanished by now. It passed through her mind and was gone.

Several people were on the streets when she arrived at Fall Creek, so named for a cascade of water pouring over a slate bluff and forming a small creek flowing past the north side of the town.

Several people waved at her and nodded as she pulled up before the bank and dismounted. She looped the reins over the hitch rail and entered the bank.

Hannah Drew, the spinster teller of the bank, saw her enter and approached the counter.

'My, Ellen, you look pretty this morning. Not that you don't always look pretty.'

'Hannah, flattery will get you most anything you want from a man, but not from me.' Ellen smiled at her. They had known each other for years. During the months the school was in session, Hannah was the teacher, building the fires in the pot-bellied stove, carrying out the ashes, and trying to impress the three R's into the minds of about a dozen children, boys and girls, coming from the town, and a few from the nearer outlying ranches.

'Is Mr Ragsdale in?' she asked Hannah, after a few minutes of casual conversation. 'I'd like to talk with him, if he is here.'

'Oh, he's back there in his office. I'll tell him you are here.'

Homer Ragsdale, always the polite man around women, rose and, coming from behind his desk, greeted Ellen.

'Miss Turner, it is always a pleasure to have you drop by. Have a seat. Would you like a cup of coffee?'

Ellen shook her head as she seated herself across the desk from him. She tried to read the man's expression, but he kept his eyes veiled, his lips in a smile. Homer Ragsdale was the wealthiest man in the territory. He had come in and established the bank and, while it was not generally known, had bought a controlling interest in the Fall Creek

Saloon. Her father had done business with Ragsdale for many seasons, and she had no reason not to continue to trust him to handle the financial part of her spread for her.

The ranch itself was not large in comparison with many of such in holdings. Ten thousand acres were nothing in relation to many of the ranches in the territory. There was plenteous water to be had and meadows that produced hay for the cattle and copses of trees for shade in the summer and protection from the winter storms. The Herefords were sneered at by many, but slowly other ranchers were beginning to envy the size and weight of her animals over the rather rangy and wild stock on their own grazes.

She settled herself across from Ragsdale and suddenly felt uneasy at the way he stared at her. She shook this off as nervousness at having to handle part of the ranch business which heretofore had been handled by her father.

Ragsdale cleared his throat. 'Just what can I do for you, Miss Turner? It goes without saying that we all were saddened at the death of your father.' He sighed and shook his head. 'Pioneers, all of them. There won't be another breed like them in the world.'

'Thank you, Mr Ragsdale,' she said. 'But life must go on and in the ranching business time waits for no one.' She shifted herself slightly and eyed him firmly.

'I need to extend my loan until my next shipment of stock. At that time I will be able to pay what I borrow now and clear up most of what my father owed you when he died.'

The banker pursed his lips and nodded. 'Yes, yes, my dear. I understand your situation. You need the money for special food for the special cattle you are raising.' He leaned back and cleared his throat. 'I have serious doubts about your enterprise. I questioned your father when he proposed buying this special breed.' He shook his head. 'Miss Turner, I am afraid you are going to lose money on this deal, and I do not like the idea of being party to an unsuccessful venture.'

She eyed him carefully. There was something sly about his glances; his expressions seemed sincere but beneath the surface, and in the tones of his conversation, she detected a wiliness that she did not understand.

'Mr Ragsdale. I need two thousand dollars to take me through to the spring shipment. By that time I will have animals that will run over a thousand pounds on the hoof. With the price of beef in the East, I should realize several dollars a pound. I anticipate a shipment that will bring no less than twenty thousand. I will be able to repay you the loan and clear what my father owed before me.'

The banker reached into a drawer, fumbled among some folders and came up with one, placing it on the desk before him. He opened it, pursed his lips and read the figures before him. He looked up at her.

'Miss Turner, your father owed the bank far more than what you would realize from your sale in the spring. On top of that your loan would push it to an impossible amount for you to handle.' He shook his head. 'I cannot see how I can venture the bank's money, which is the money of your neighboring ranchers, in loaning you more. In fact, a payment on the amount owed presently is almost due.'

'But I need that food for the cattle, to assure their getting through the winter without too much weight-loss. When spring roundup comes, they could be in good weight for shipment.'

He slowly shook his head. 'I am afraid not, Miss Turner. In fact, I should have a payment on your current debt before I even consider adding another loan. No, I cannot see my way clear to giving you the loan. And,' he glanced down at the paper before him. 'There is a payment due in six weeks on the old loan.'

Suddenly she was deeply shaken. She had never considered that the banker would not give her the loan. And now, demanding a payment on her father's account. She straightened, her face pale, but set with determination.

'I will get through the winter somehow without your help,' she said firmly. 'And I will make the payment on the existing account before payment is due.' With that she rose and turning her back on the banker walked out of the office. She did not see the sly smile that crept over Ragsdale's face as she left. He leaned back in his chair and still smiling, lighted a cigar, reflecting on the past few minutes.

* * *

Blue spent the night rolled in his blankets in the livery. Rising early, he tended to his horse and then, dousing his face in a nearby horse-trough, he went to the small restaurant. With a full breakfast under his belt he decided it was time to visit a few of the ranches nearby to see if they needed a hand for the upcoming Fall roundup. He led his horse from the livery and was tightening the cinch when a voice yelled back of him.

'All right now! You've got your iron on. Turn around and face me like a man!'

Blue looked across the saddle of his horse and saw Eli, the ranny he had fought the day before. He stepped around the horse and faced him.

'I want no trouble with you,' he said. 'We had our little dance yesterday. Now, let it go.'

'Not before I even it up with you,' snarled Eli. Early as it was, Blue could see that the man was liquored up. 'No man bests me, fists or guns, more than once. Now, step out away from your hoss and let's see just how much sand you've got. Or does the idea of a gunfight chill you?'

Blue sighed. Always there seemed to be someone challenging the other man with a gun. True, the story of his exploits in the Rimrock war in Arizona had moved on ahead of him. But that was long ago. All he wanted now was a job, a place to finally settle down. Maybe raise a family.

He stepped away from his horse. 'There's no need of this, Eli,' he said. 'I don't fear you, but I don't like to draw my gun just because someone says so. For the last time, let it go.' As he spoke Blue stepped away from his horse.

'No way. You draw, or run!' Eli stood a hundred feet away, legs straddled, right hand paused, quivering above his gun butt.

'Draw! he yelled and his hand slashed down toward his pistol.

3

Ellen Turner stepped from the bank onto the boardwalk and paused, her face startled as she looked at the tableau coming into focus in the main street of the town. A few feet away she saw Mel Lewis, her foreman, slouched against a post, his eyes fastened upon the scene before him. Seeing his boss emerge from the bank, he straightened as though to turn and go into the saloon, but shrugged and leaned back against the post. She had already seen him. He might as well stay where he was.

One of her cowhands, one called Eli, was facing a man, a stranger to her and as she realized her rannie was in the fight, she gasped as his hand slashed down to his gun-butt.

Blue had faced Eli, realizing that there was nothing else he could do. The man was determined to gun him down, if possible. On the periphery of his sight he saw the woman standing, her hands at her mouth, watch the scene in the street. Fleetingly he was sorry she was to see what was about to happen, but there was nothing he could do about it now. Eli was drawing!

As the blue-steel barrel of Eli's pistol cleared the top of the holster, Blue drew and turning sideways to the gunman, leveled his own pistol, cocking the hammer as he did so. Eli's sixgun roared and a slug whistled by Blue's ear. Cursing, Eli thumbed back his pistol hammer again and lined up with Blue.

Blue's pistol roared. Through the smoke Blue saw a splash of red appear on Eli's vest. The eyes glared and Eli dropped his weapon and grappled at his chest. Rising on his toes. he staggered and then fell, to pour out his life's blood in the dust of the street.

Blue stood, his sixgun in his hand at his side, looking at the inert body of his opponent. Eli had shown that he was no gunman. His draw was slow, and his shot was fired erratically, missing Blue by inches. A sad look passed over Blue's countenance. He had not wished the fight, but it had been pushed to such limits that he had nothing to do but retaliate. Slowly he raised his pistol and, punching the empty shell from the cylinder, slipped a fresh one into the empty slot. He slid the weapon into his holster and swung into his saddle. Once again, he noticed the young woman standing with pale face, large eyes staring at him. He turned his horse and rode out of the town.

Ellen Turner watched him leave. She had seen enough of the fight to realize that Eli had forced it. Yet she deeply resented the seeming coolness of the man riding out of the town. He had committed a crime, surely, and was riding away from it.

She turned to the banker. 'That man simply shot my rider, and rode away and no one did anything about it. Can't you get the town marshal to arrest him? Or the sheriff of the territory?'

Ragsdale shook his head. 'There's no town marshal. The sheriff is in Pierre and when he is told the circumstances, he won't do anything. In fact, there is nothing he can do.'

'What do you mean, nothing he can do?'

'There were witnesses who know your man picked a fight with that man. Blue, he said his name was. Picked on him in the saloon. Blue whipped him in a fist-fight. Today, Eli challenged him and then drew first. He fired first, missed, and the stranger fired one time.' He shrugged. 'He was just protecting himself and Eli was to blame, causing both the fist-fight and the gunfight you just saw.'

Ellen turned and looked quickly at the saloon. She had seen Mel Lewis standing there, leaning against a porch post. Now he was gone. What was he doing in town? Hoppy had told her Lewis was in the back pastures checking on the herd there. She shook her head. Something was going on that she did not understand. She would have a talk with the foreman.

She turned to the banker. 'Mr Ragsdale, if you will take care of Eli, have the undertaker to care for the body, I will pay whatever costs there are. He may have ER's horse and tack and whatever is on the body. If there is further costs, let me know and I will take care of it.' Ragsdale nodded.

She then went into the mercantile where she purchased a few items and, returning to her horse, thrust them into a saddle-bag. She mounted and rode out of town. Her mind was caught up in the scene of her hand, Eli, being killed before her eyes. And the fact that her foreman was not where he was supposed to be.

* * *

Blue left the trail that led out of town and apparently headed toward the ranches in the area. Instead of following the beaten route, he turned into a path apparently seldom used, seeing that there were only a few tracks, which led upward into the lift of the foothills of the Black Hills. He wished to get higher where he might survey the area about him, getting an idea of the layout of the land. He was a stranger here and such knowledge might be useful in the future. His horse climbed the ill-defined trail easily, and in a short while the path opened into a clearing with a clear view of the land about him.

He dismounted and loosened the cinch, dropped the reins on the horse's neck and allowed him to graze on an abundance of grass in the clearing. He climbed higher to a small prominence and surveyed the area about him. Before him spread out miles of good cattle-land, much graze, copses of trees for shade and protection during the winter months. In the distance he saw buildings and surmised them to be the headquarters of a ranch.

It was a fair land and he felt tempted to remain where he was, find a small ranch he might buy. Get some cattle and start his own herd. Maybe somewhere find a woman willing to share her life with him, and with her raise a family. Wistfully he thought of all this as he looked over the richness of the land before him.

His horse snorted and he turned to look where it grazed. It stood with head up, ears pricked forward. Then Blue heard the brushing of foliage against the movement of a horse or man. He stood and waited, listening. The sounds became louder, and then suddenly a horse carrying a rider broke into the clearing.

The rider was slumped over in the saddle, his hands clutching the saddle horn. The horse stopped and looked at Blue's mount standing amid the lush grass of the clearing. The rider moaned and suddenly began to slide from the saddle.

Blue moved forward swiftly and

catching the man as he slipped downward, lowered him gently to the ground. Quickly he removed the saddle-bags from the horse and, draping the reins over the horse's neck, slapped it on the flank. The animal joined Blue's horse among the lush grasses and began grazing.

Blue knelt beside the man. There was blood on his left leg and the man opened his eyes as Blue turned the leg so he could see the seriousness of the wound. Taking his knife, he slit the trouser leg and grimaced as he saw the torn flesh where the slug had entered and then ripped its way through, emerging to leave a mangled exit site. The man groaned.

'Who're you?' he grunted, attempting to rise.

Blue gently pushed him back to the ground. 'You'd best lay still, until I get a tourniquet about that leg of yours. You've got a pretty good wound there.'

The man groaned again as Blue slit the trouser leg further and then, taking the man's kerchief from about his neck, twisted it tightly above the wound. The bleeding slowed down and then stopped.

'My name is Blue, if that's any consolation to you. You came busting out of the brush there and fell off your horse. And, friend, you have a pretty nasty leg there.'

'Guess I was where I hadn't ought to have been,' the man said. 'I was goin' to a ranch, cuttin' across country, an' first thing I knowed there was men shootin' at me.'

'Well, let's get you on your hoss and see if there's a ranch nearby where we can bind you up better, and maybe get a doctor out to see you.'

'I saw a house an' some sheds, back there, not far frum here,' the man grunted. He looked up at Blue. 'My name's Noah . . . Noah Fitzgerald.' His pain-filled eyes searched Blue's face. 'If you are thinkin' I'm somebody's escaped slave, Mr Blue, you are wrong. My old master freed all his slaves afore the war. But I stayed by my missis until the war was over. There was nothin' fer me to stay there for, so I come west. Been driftin' from ranch to ranch, roundup to roundup. I just now run into some trouble an' I don't know fer sure just what I done wrong.'

Blue wrapped his own kerchief about the leg over the wound. He nodded. 'That war is over with now, and we are men together. I'll get you to that house and maybe we can get a doctor.'

He rose and gathered the reins of Noah's horse and brought it up beside the man. Helping him to his one good leg, Blue boosted Noah into the saddle. Noah groaned with the pain of the action, but clung grimly to the saddle horn.

Blue brought his own horse, mounted and took the reins of the wounded man's horse. 'Just what direction would you say that house is that you saw?' he asked.

Noah raised his hand and pointed. 'Back that way for a mile or so. But they may not want to help out a black man.'

'They'll help,' Blue said grimly. Leading the one horse, he left the clearing, working his way in the direction Noah had pointed. Behind him the black man groaned with pain as brush swept across his leg, and the constant motion of the horse made him sway. Sweat stood out upon his face, and his teeth were clenched at the pain. He hung onto the saddle horn with both hands, enduring the ride.

Lifting across a small roll in the land, the brush and pines thinning, Blue saw the house and sheds Noah had spoken of. He nodded toward them.

'Is that the spread you saw?' The black man raised his pain-filled eyes and looked where Blue pointed.

'Yeah, that's it,' he said.

Blue gigged his horse gently and led the wounded man through the brush and trees, finding in a few minutes a worn trail that led down out of the woods toward the barn lot of the ranch. There were some cattle in a nearby pasture that looked strange to Blue, he being used to the range cattle that were usually seen, sometimes mixed with the Texas longhorn breed. These cattle were stockier and fuller of body than the ones he was used to seeing.

He led Noah toward the front of the house and pulled up before a hitching rail. He dismounted and looped the reins of his horse over it, then led the other to the rail and did the same. He came back to Noah and taking hold of the man's arm and body, gently eased him from the saddle. As he did so an oldster appeared from what was the cook-shack and called to them.

'Hey, thar. Who're you all?' He came toward them. Blue eased Noah onto the porch of the house and the wounded man sighed with relief at being out of the saddle. He leaned back against a post. Blue turned to the questioner.

'That feller looks like he needs some takin' care of,' the old man said. 'I'm Hoppy Jackson, the spread's cook. I'm the only one here right now. The boys are out checkin' the cattle and some brakes where they might get broke legs. Miss Turner, the boss, is in town.'

'Miss Turner? Your boss is a woman?' Blue said quizzically.

'Yeah. An' she's doing a good job of runnin' the spread,' the cook informed them. 'Her pa was shot and killed about six months ago. She's been runnin' it since.' He eyed Noah critically.

'I think we best get this darkie over to the bunkhouse. There's an empty bunk there. I'm not a sawbones, but I've took a lot of bullets outta rannies that got in the way of 'em. If I think it's too bad fer me to work on, we'll just have to ride into town and get old Doc Buttler to have a go at him.'

With Noah between them, they took him to the bunkhouse and laid him on an empty bunk. Hoppy lighted some lamps and moved a table close to the cot, placing the lamps on it so the light would illuminate the wound as he worked. He got a quart bottle of whiskey and placed it beside the bunk.

'I'll have to wash it out with this here liquor. It's a shame to waste good booze on doctorin', but it's the best we can do. Now, let's get them pants off and take him outta them long johns so's I can get a good look at that wound.'

Stripped, Noah lay back, groaning as the old cowboy pressed, poked and prodded about the wound. Hoppy muttered and talked as he worked.

'The bullet went all the way through. Fer as I kin see there was no arteries cut nor bones smashed. I think that cleaning the wound and stitching it up a little, he'll heal right away. But he'll have to be off it fer two or three weeks.' Hoppy straightened and looked at Blue. 'Where did you say he got shot at?'

Blue looked at Noah. 'Just where were you when you was shot?' he asked.

Noah opened his eyes. His face twisted in pain for a moment before he answered.

'It's hard to figure out, layin' like this

and havin' someone poking around in your leg. Ahhh . . . that smarts good bit,' he told Hoppy. The cook did not answer, but continued to explore the wound for threads that might have been carried into it by the slug.

'I was ridin' over a ridge, about, say . . . three miles or a little more from here. I started down off the high point of the ridge toward a little creek at the bottom, to water my hoss. I'd got about half-way down the slope when someone shot at me. I turned my hoss and started back the way I had come, and they shot again and this time got me in the leg. That's about all I can remember until I fell off my hoss an' you found me.'

'There's a little creek about four miles from here,' grunted Cookie, rising up from the leg. 'It's on the ST ranch.'

'Could it have been any of the men working on this ranch?' asked Blue.

Hoppy shrugged. 'I can't see any of our boys shootin' someone just passin' through. I'd say it was not one of them.'

'One of who?' asked another voice. Blue turned to look at a burly, bearded man, who stepped into the bunkhouse.

'What's goin' on here, and just who are you two?'

4

Nathan Wolfgang was the owner of the sprawling N slash W spread, that was comprised over fifty thousand acres of land and grazing territory owned by the government. The government land was free grazing for anyone needing the support beyond their proven-up holdings. But as far as Wolfgang was concerned, only his cattle and horses, bearing the N slash W brand, were to feed off the lush grasses of the prairies he claimed.

A small, narrow-shouldered man, his small lean face twisted in a constant frown, Wolfgang ruled his domain with a stingy and iron hand. Cattle not bearing his brand were driven off, at times killed and left for scavengers. If squatters appeared and claimed land about a creek or a spring, they were rousted off the land, their tents and wagons burned, their animals confiscated. Any newcomers who fought against his army of men were brutally killed and left for others to bury. There was no law closer than Pierre. The owner of the N slash W had a clear hand in whatever he decided was right by his reasoning. And his reasoning and logic were that all he desired was his for the taking.

One day he stood on a hill slope, beneath a huge pine, and looked out over the valley and level meadows that belonged to the ST ranch. His eyes glinted. This was a prime object. There was a creek winding an erratic way through the spread. There were springs situated here and there, which was important to any rancher with herds. There were good copses of piñon and pine, here and there large water-oaks, forming shelter during the winter and shade in the heat of the summer. It was a treasure. Small, only a few acres proven up as actual holding, undoubtedly filed in Pierre years ago. The rest of the area was government land, with freedom to graze as needed.

He nodded to himself. It was a jewel. Water, shelter, grass, all a rancher needed. And, with his hundreds of cattle and as many horses, there was not enough graze or water on the N slash W. He had to have this ten thousand acres.

It had come to him that the owner of the ST — a girl, actually — was pushed for cash needed to tide her through to the spring roundup. She was attempting to raise a different brand of cattle, which was an experimental project. Heavier cattle? More beef per animal? He shook his head. It was an improbable attempt in this area, where the winters were long and hard. Not born to the rigours of the elements, these animals would not make it. Perhaps it was time to give her something to think about.

He mounted his horse and rode back to his ranch, his mind caught up with a plan to acquire that land, and get rid of an impediment to his increasing the size of his operation, achieving more water and graze. It was time to have a talk with Homer Ragsdale.

* * *

Mel Lewis stood glaring at Blue, and the figure of Noah, a black cowboy, stretched out upon the bunk. Hoppy, straightening from examining Noah's leg, glanced at the foreman.

'We got a wounded boy here, Mel. I'm tryin' to see just how bad his leg is.'

Lewis turned his gaze to Blue. 'I saw you in town today. I don't want you on this spread. Now, take your so-called wounded buddy and get off this place.' He turned to leave, then halted.

Ellen Turner stepped through the door. She surveyed the tableau before her and her glance fell on Noah, his face twisted in pain from Hoppy's poking and prodding at the wound.

Her expression softened. 'Hoppy, what is the situation here? Who is the man whose leg you seem to be removing from his body?'

Hoppy straightened up. 'Miss Ellen, this here cowboy has a real bad leg. I think it'll be all right, fer the bullet went clear through. I'm just cleanin' it up some and then I'll bind it good. He oughtta be up and around in two, three weeks.'

She approached the bunk and looked down into Noah's face. 'You may stay here until you can ride, cowboy. We don't turn wounded men out just because they are strangers.' She straightened up and looked at Blue.

'I know who you are. Blue, the banker said was your name. You killed one of my riders today at Fall Creek. I saw it.'

Blue nodded, removing his hat as he did so. His eyes met her gaze calmly.

'Yes, ma'am. I shot a man in town this morning. I didn't know he was one of your riders. But, if you saw it happen you know that he drew on me first. I protected myself.' His eyes did not waver from hers.

She sighed. 'I hate killing and to see it right in front of your eyes makes it real and worse. But he did draw his gun and he was firing when you drew your gun.' She shuddered at the thought and then suddenly turned to the foreman.

'Hoppy told me you were out scouting the place where my father was killed. Did you find anything that would point to the killer?'

Lewis shook his head. 'I didn't see a thing. Lots of tracks of them what came and examined the area before.' He started to leave.

'Lewis.' Her voice crackled with a sudden anger. He turned back. He looked at her questioningly.

'You just lied to me.' There was a deep run of anger in her voice.

His face tightened. 'Miss Turner, them are fightin' words if they come from a man. Just why don't you believe what I told you?'

'Because you were standing, leaning against a post on the saloon veranda and saw this man shoot Eli Whitted. I saw you there. You couldn't have been in two places at the same time.'

'That is a mighty hard thing to accuse a man of,' he said bitterly. 'You must have seen someone wearin' about the garb as I wear.'

She was silent a moment and then turned to Blue. 'Are you looking for a job?'

She opened her eyes and saw Blue directly for the first time since she had seen him in the gunfight. He was over six feet tall, straight, indicating military training during the last war. His eyes were grey-blue, and his expression at the moment non-committal, but she noticed laugh wrinkles about his eyes, and his lips were full and easily turned to a smile. Obviously a contained individual, he had shown no overt reaction to the foreman's attitude toward him and the negro soldier.

He searched her face for a moment and then nodded. 'I'm hoping to find a job somewhere in the area. I like this part of the country, and my father settled not far from here.'

She did not shift her gaze. Suddenly she liked what she saw and, much like her father before her, she made an instant decision.

'Very well. I'm short a hand, as you now know. You can sign on so long as your friend needs to rest up and heal. Then we'll talk about a longer term, if I like your work.'

A wry smile twisted his mouth and he chuckled. 'Miss Turner, that is the strangest hiring I have ever heard. But it's fair, and I will accept — for the time being, that is.'

The foreman broke in with a curse. 'Look, boss, I'm foreman and I hire and fire whoever I think to. If you — '

She faced him, her face stern and her voice sharp. 'You *were* foreman, Lewis. I will not tolerate a liar. I find that I cannot trust you.'

Lewis's face mottled with a rush of blood and he glared at her.

'Woman — ' he began and clenching

his fists he took a step toward her. Quickly Blue pushed the young woman aside and stood before the foreman, his body relaxed, his eyes alert and boring into those of the man.

'Just as I reckoned. You're the kind that ain't afraid of women and children. Now, how about me? You want to take me on?'

Lewis stepped back and crouched, his right hand poising over his gun-butt, the fingers splayed and trembling.

'I ain't afraid of any man, an' I wasn't goin' to hurt her.' Realizing his situation he ceased talking. Women were revered in the Western territories. They were a lot fewer than men, and were often sent for by advertisements in Eastern newspapers. They were treated with courtesy and respect. Lewis knew he had stepped beyond the code and now he blustered to rescue himself from a mistake that the entire community would scorn.

'I think you owe Miss Turner an apology,' Blue said softly, 'or step outside with me.'

Lewis dropped his hand away from his pistol. He nodded to his former employer. 'Sorry, Miss Turner. I just lost my head for a moment. I meant you no harm.'

'Couldn't tell it by yer actions,' grunted Hoppy. 'Why don't you draw your pay an' get!'

Lewis eyed them all sullenly for a long moment and then brought his attention back to Blue.

'Me'n you will get this settled one day soon, mark my words.'

He jerked around and walked swiftly out of the building.

Ellen Turner bit her lip as she watched the foreman leave the room. She was silent a moment, then looked up at Blue. She hesitated a moment before speaking, her voice suddenly tired from the confrontation with Lewis.

'I don't want you to find trouble on my account,' she said softly. 'But I do thank you for what you did.' She reached out and touched his arm. She felt the strength through the fabric of his shirt and suddenly she was warm inside. It had been a long time since she had had someone near her own age with whom to talk. Slowly, her hand returned to her side. She turned, suddenly unnerved at her feeling.

'How is your patient, Hoppy?' She stepped closer and looked down at Noah with a smile. 'I'm Ellen Turner. I am the owner of the ST ranch. You are welcome to stay here as long as necessary while you are recuperating.'

The black man nodded politely. 'My name is Noah Fitzgerald, ma'am,' he said. 'And thank you for your kindness. This Hoppy here may not be a doctor, but I'm grateful for his lookin' after my leg. However, I have a feeling he's better at healin' hurt hosses, than human beings.' A twinkle was in his eyes.

She laughed quietly. 'I won't venture to even discuss that,' she said, whimsically. 'But he is a good cook, as you will find out before long.'

She went to the door and then paused, looking at Blue. 'Hoppy will fill you in. There are four other hands who will be in for supper and you can meet them. When you get a chance, come on up to the house and we will talk terms.'

* * *

In his nicely appointed office in the rear of the bank, Homer Ragsdale and Nathan Wolfgang sat across from each other, Ragsdale behind the desk, the rancher on the other side. Wolfgang was the kind of man who would not relax when approaching a business deal. He sat on the edge of a solid, straight-backed chair, holding his hat on his lap, staring with expressionless face across the desk at the banker.

'Mr Ragsdale,' he said, his mean little face screwed up in a scowl. 'I think, under the circumstances, that it is time you and I discussed the possibility of removing the ST ranch as an obstacle to any future plans between myself and your institution.'

5

In a month Noah was riding again. His leg was healed and he was eager to show his appreciation to 'Miss Ellen' as everyone called her. It was then the ST owner called Blue into her office in the main house.

She pointed to a chair and seated herself behind her desk. Since the strange stirring in her mind and body as she touched him, she had held herself almost rigidly apart from him. Now she looked at him levelly, her emotions under control.

'You've made a very good hand, Blue,' she told him, her eyes holding his own with steady gaze. 'I've watched you and liked your work. I like especially how you handled that young yearling I had just bought. He looks like good material.'

Blue nodded. 'He's a good horse,

Miss Ellen, got a lot of promise.'

'How do you like working here at the ST?' she asked. 'I am short a hand, as you know. If you want the job, it's yours. At the same rate I was paying you during the time Noah was healing. How is he coming along?'

'He's going to ride a little with me today,' Blue answered. 'We both thank you for your consideration. And to answer your other question. Yes, I'd like a job with you and thirty a month and found is fine with me, and I'm sure it will be with Noah, if you can afford to keep him on.'

She nodded, smiling. 'Roundup is due. I will need an extra hand during that time. After roundup, we'll see about his staying on.

'By the way,' she added. 'If you are going to work for me, what do I put on the books for your name? Surely it is more than just 'Blue'.'

He smiled, rose, and took up his hat. 'Ma'am, Blue will have to do for now. Just call me Blue and put it on the books that way.'

She shrugged. 'Very well, as you wish. Do you think you might go to the pastures over by the mesa and check on the beef over there? In fact, if Noah is going to ride some today, perhaps he might go along.'

Blue nodded and moved to the door. 'I'll ask him. And again, my thanks for both of us.'

* * *

It was painful for Noah to mount, but once mounted the pain in his leg subsided and he rode along with Blue, enjoying his first outing and looking about him.

'This is nice land,' he remarked. 'Water and shelter and graze. I don't know anything about the kind of cattle she is trying to raise, but if good grazing and land to fatten them on is all that's needed, I'd say the layout is about right for any kind of critter.'

The morning was well along when

finally they reached the mesa area. Blue saw immediately that it was indeed an ideal place for fattening cattle of any kind. It was not long before they saw a field of grazing animals, showing the black-and-white colouring of the Herefords the ST ranch was experimenting with.

Moving around the brakes and meadows of lush grass, Blue and Noah counted somewhere in the neighborhood of eight or nine hundred head of the cattle, all well fattened out for the coming winter months. With their survey completed they started back to the ranch headquarters.

The sun was slanting toward the rims of the surrounding hills when they breasted the last rise and paused, overlooking the ranch. Blue immediately saw a group of horsemen before the main house, and the figure of Ellen Turner talking with them. A run of suspicion raced through his body. She had not mentioned any such visitors. In fact, the stance of the one talking with her was one of stiffness, or suppressed anger.

'You stay here,' he told Noah. 'Something's not right down there. I'll move around and come in from the back of the barns. I think the boss may need some support.'

Noah nodded. 'I'll watch, an' if you'all need help, wave a hat an' I'll come runnin'.'

Blue rode back beyond sight of anyone talking with Ellen Turner, and moved about so that he approached back of the barn and corrals. He dismounted and walked casually but quietly until he stood at one corner of the house.

* * *

Nathan Wolfgang sat on his thoroughbred stallion looking down at Ellen Turner.

'Miss Turner, I am offering you a handsome amount for your spread, such as it is. It is not fully developed.

You are running less than a thousand head of beef on all this area. You are tying up good water and graze for a few animals of dubious breed. All your neighbors are doubting your success. When you fail, and I am certain you will, what will you do? Sell out for a song to the first bidder for your spread? That is not good business. So you should seriously consider my offer.'

Ellen looked up at him, her face animated.

'Mr Wolfgang I do take you seriously. I have given you my answer. I won't sell the ST ranch to you or anyone else. Now, please leave my ranch.'

Wolfgang's foreman was one Sam Fletcher. A huge man, cold in his attitude to everyone, he glared down at the slight, erect woman before them.

'Boss,' he said, pausing to squirt a mouthful of tobacco juice into a flower-bed before the veranda, 'Let's just cut the palaver. Let me talk to her a minute, an' I'll persuade her to your way of thinkin'.' He started to dismount, then paused, half-way out of his saddle.

'Miss Turner,' Blue drawled, stepping around the corner of the house and looking up at her. 'I got that little job done you set me to. Is there anything else right now?'

Before she could answer, Nathan Wolfgang turned his eyes on Blue.

'You are interfering in something that is none of your business, whoever you are,' Wolfgang said. 'What I have to say is for Miss Turner alone.'

'Not necessarily,' Ellen Turner said. 'This man is the foreman of my ranch. He and I have no secrets so far as the ranch is concerned.'

Wolfgang glared at her and then at her just-that-moment created foreman of the ST, an appointment of which he was unaware.

'What is your name?'

Blue eyed him coolly. 'I'm called Blue. And as you should know, out here it is discourteous to ask a man's moniker without reason.'

Sam Fletcher spoke, 'Boss, just let me get off and dance a set or two with this rannie. Maybe I can change his tune somewhat.' He moved as though to dismount.

Only Ellen saw the lightning-fast movement of Blue's right hand. One moment it was hanging by his side. The next moment it was filled with a sixgun, the yawning maw pointed at Wolfgang's belt buckle.

'If he sets one foot on the ground,' Blue's steely voice ripped through the air, 'you will get a slug in your gut. Now get that man back in his saddle. All of you put your hands on your saddle horns. And Mr Whatever *your* name is, you are about one second away from an untimely death!'

Fletcher made as though to step from his saddle. As the gun in Blue's hand was cocked, the metallic click echoed against the side of the house. Nathan Wolfgang paled.

'Fletcher! Damn you! Stay in that

saddle!' Wolfgang's voice rasped with anger and nervousness. The sight of that sixgun held steadily upon him was more than he could take.

There were six men with him and, with the exception of the foreman, they were all sitting with hands folded and on their saddle horns. The gun in the hand of this cold-eyed rannie was enough for them to do as they were told.

'Mr Wolfgang,' Ellen said, looking the old man steadily in the face. 'We have completed our business, such as it was. Now, please leave my ranch, before this grows more serious.'

Wolfgang reined his horse around. 'You haven't heard the last of this, Miss Turner!' he spat out, as though her name was distasteful. 'You will be begging for my aid before long, mark my words. And when that time comes I probably will not be as easy to deal with as now.'

With that he gigged his horse and led his crew out of the yard. Sam Fletcher, the foreman of the N slash W ranch paused before Blue.

'You best be shakin' the dust of this country off your boots,' he said. 'The country ain't big enough for both of us.'

Blue had holstered his pistol. He stood in an easy stance, his eyes meeting Fletcher's gaze.

'I'll be around,' he said softly. 'Ain't seen anything yet to scare me away.'

'I'll see you again,' growled Fletcher. 'Real soon.' With that he spurred his horse and raced from the yard to catch up with the rest of his crew.

Ellen Turner looked at Blue with troubled eyes. 'I always seem to be getting you into trouble on my account. Thank you. I was glad to see you come around the corner. Thanks for keeping the NW foreman in his saddle.'

'All in a day's work, ma'am,' said Blue. As he walked away the thought came to him that here was a marriageable young woman, nice-looking and with a good head on her shoulders. She would make someone an excellent wife.

He almost halted in his tracks. A wife? A feeling ran through him. For the first time in a long time he looked upon a woman and realized his feeling toward her was more than admiration — he was attracted to her. He shook his head and moved on. But through the day during his working hours, she appeared in his thoughts again and again.

* * *

With roundup on them, the crew for the ST spread was pushed to gather up the cattle on the wide spaces of the ranch. Brakes were scoured, cul-de-sacs searched. The herd from the meadows on the edge of the mesa was brought in. It was hard, hot work, dangerous for horse and man, but on the day the roundup was to begin, Blue was satisfied that the Herefords were ready for the count and branding of calves.

As they gathered up the herd off the ST ranch, naturally there were other brands that had drifted into the area.

These were cut from the Herefords and hazed into the holding area of the brand indicated. It was at the end of the second day that Sam Fletcher, foreman for the N slash W spread appeared at the edge of the fire where Ellen and Hoppy were busy preparing the evening meal for the crew.

Blue, checking the remuda, saw Fletcher approaching. He stepped away from the horses and faced the foreman without speaking.

Fletcher paused just past the chuck-wagon, watching Blue approaching.

'Wa'al, I told you we'd meet again. Now, before we begin our confab, there's someone I want you to meet. I've told him about you and he thinks he knows you.'

A tall figure stepped up beside Fletcher from the gathering darkness.

He was slender almost to the point of being skinny. His face was bony, with a long nose and gimlet eyes buried deeply beneath shaggy eyebrows. His lips were a compressed slit in his mouth, as though they had never known a smile.

He stared at Blue. His hands automatically reached to the blackened butts of two sixguns strapped to each side. A two-gun killer, thought Blue, and mean and traitorous.

'Howdy, Blue. It's been a long time.' The voice was coarse, raspy, as though seldom used.

Blue nodded coolly. 'Howdy, Bob. It has been a long time, but so far as I am concerned, not long enough. What brings you here to the Black Hills?'

'Why, there's gold in them hills,' the man said. 'I reckoned on getting me some of it before it is all gone.'

'Then I suggest you get at it, and leave us here to our work.'

The man shook his head slowly. 'No. Bob Jenkins lets nothing keep him from paying a debt. In this case, getting my just dues, from a stinking sheepherder what helped kill a lot of my friends in the Rimrock fracas down in Arizona a while back.'

Blue shifted his stance. This man

was unpredictable. Talking soft one moment, and grabbing for his guns and blazing away the next. Blue remembered him from that unhappy time but a few years ago. Jenkins would sell his guns to the highest bidder, and there was no emotion whatsoever in killing.

'I'm told that you are foreman for this small spread that is tryin' to raise some outlandish critters. An' that you killed a man in cold blood in town just because he didn't see things your way. Now, some of his friends think you should have your come-uppance an' have asked me to take care of it.'

Blue looked at him and said nothing. What was there to say? This man was sent here to kill him, and this was his way of going about it.

Jenkins stepped further into the light of the camp-fire. Behind him Fletcher grinned and stepped aside. Ellen stood, horrified that such a challenge should come about.

'I saw the shooting.' She stepped forward between the two men. 'Eli

Whitted went for his gun, drew and fired, before this man drew to protect himself — '

'Lady,' intoned Jenkins, 'just step out of the way. No matter what you say, I'm here to do a job. I don't want to hurt you, but I will, if I have to. Now, move!' His voice cracked and Ellen stiffened.

Blue stepped to her and touched her arm. 'Let me handle this, Miss Ellen. You can't talk this man out of it. He's a killer, sent to do a job. You just step back there beside Hoppy and I'll see what I can do with this man.'

Blue faced Jenkins, without speaking. His eyes narrowed and he stood relaxed, his right hand hanging loosely by his side.

'Jenkins, this doesn't have to happen. Let it go. I want no trouble with you.'

Jenkins slowly shook his head. 'Go for your iron, Blue! I've waited a long time to see if you are as good as the tales they tell about you in Arizona rimrock country.'

6

Mel Lewis sat across a table from Homer Ragsdale, the banker of Fall Creek. The saloon was nearly empty this early in the day. Lewis fiddled with his glass of beer and listened to the banker.

'Are the ST beef in a place likely not to be found by anyone hunting them? I want to get them to a railhead as soon after roundup as possible.'

Lewis nodded. 'Yup. Won't no one find them. Besides, they are across the line from the ST on the N slash W spread.'

Startled, the banker looked at Lewis directly. 'On Wolfgang's land? Does he know it?'

Lewis shook his head. 'Nope. An' if we move pretty quick, he won't ever know. Then, if someone finds them afore we ship them, they'll blame

Wolfgang, probably accuse him of rustlin'.'

Ragsdale smiled. 'Very well. Now, how about that other thing I set you to do? Did you find anything?'

Lewis fiddled with the glass again, lifted it up for a swallow and motioned for Higgens, the bartender, to bring him another beer. He sat quiet until the drink was before him and Ragsdale also had a refill of his whiskey. He sipped his beer and eyed the banker. 'Just how much is in this for me if I locate the . . . site?'

The banker stirred irritably. 'I've already told you. Your part will depend upon how much you find and the quality of the find.'

Lewis brooded. Finally he eyed the banker directly with steady eyes over the rim of his beer glass.

'Ragsdale, I am a suspicious rannie. I take very few men's words for final deals. I won't even take a handshake. Put it on paper so it can be read by anyone, signed by you. When you've done that, we can talk again. Not until.'

He rose, finished his beer with a gulp and noisily set the mug on the table. He turned his back on the banker and left the saloon.

Ragsdale sat for a long time, angry, frustrated. He was unused to being ordered about in his dealings with other men. But he could see that Mel Lewis was not only cagey, but determined. He finished his drink, waved to Higgens and left. He returned to his office mulling over the situation with the former ST ranch foreman. He would find a way of learning what Lewis knew, one way or another.

* * *

The firelight glinted on the sixgun as Jenkins slapped his hand down, wrapped his fingers about the butt of his pistol and drew it quickly from the holster.

Ellen Turner had seen Blue draw his weapons twice before this occasion. Her face pale, she stepped further away from the fire. Vaguely she saw Hoppy go to the chuck-wagon for something and then fade back into the darkness. Her attention was fastened upon the tableau building before her.

Blue's hand flashed down and up and, as Jenkins's weapon cleared leather, blasted in roar and smoke! Jenkins's slug whistled past Blue's head. Jenkins was staggering and yelling, then he collapsed as Blue's bullet fractured his right hip. From the ground, Jenkins twisted around and attempted once more to fire, but Blue's second bullet drilled him through the shoulder. He was flung backwards to the ground and lay groaning with pain and frustration.

Sam Fletcher, the N slash W foreman, cursed as he saw Jenkins go down. He slapped his hand down upon his pistol butt and felt a hard object bore into his back.

'Make one move to draw that iron an' there'll be a hole in you to drive a burro through.' Hoppy Jackson's voice grated on his ear. 'Now, pull it out real slow with two fingers, and drop it on the ground.' Fletcher heard the ominous click of a shotgun-hammer being thumbed back.

Glaring at Blue through the smoke drifting between them, Fletcher did as ordered. Hoppy pushed him into the circle of the camp-fire's light.

'This rannie was thinkin' of joinin' in this here dance, but I dissuaded him,' he called over to Blue.

Blue fastened his cold eyes upon the foreman.

'Punch out his shells, Hoppy, and give him back his pistol. You,' he addressed Fletcher, 'get yourself back to your outfit, taking that varmint there with you.' He gestured to Jenkins.

'If you set him on me,' he further said to Fletcher, 'you had better be ready the next time you try it. I'll come at you first, then take care of whoever you send against me.'

Fletcher did not answer, but glaring at Blue and then Hoppy, he shoved his empty pistol into his holster. He pulled a groaning Jenkins to his one good leg and staggered with him to a horse. He shoved the wounded man into the saddle, mounted and led Jenkins away in the darkness.

Tired from the tension and stress of the moment, Ellen turned and stepped into the darkness formed by the canvas top of the cook-wagon. She bumped into someone and, startled, stepped back.

'It's just me,' Blue's voice said to her. 'I got out of the firelight so I would no longer be a target.' He stared down into her face. 'Are you all right?'

She sniffled, beginning to relax after seeing Blue's hand flash down and, impossibly fast, rise with a blasting sixgun. She shuddered and suddenly weak, sank against him.

Protectingly, his arms went about her and gathered her close to his side. She seemed to melt into him, and for long moments he stirred at the touch of her warm, womanly body. Without realizing what he was doing, he tilted her chin and kissed her gently. For a moment her lips resisted, and then moved softly beneath his own. Sweet, soft lips, returning his kiss . . .

She jerked away and leaning back in his arms, looked up into his face. 'I . . . I'm sorry. I didn't mean to . . .'

He slowly released her and she stepped away. 'If necessary, Ellen, I apologize,' Blue said softly.

She looked up at him, her face shadowed by the wagon-top. But she felt his deeper breathing, and remembered the sincerity of his kiss. She had had many cowboys, business men and boys she had grown up with come to her in her maturity and seek her favours. Other than to accompany one to a dance in Fall Creek, now and then, she had little interest in men. But this was different. She drew away slightly, her hand reaching up to caress his cheek.

'It isn't necessary,' she murmured. 'It was nice.' She continued to look into his face and then, turning, she sought her blankets beneath the chuck-wagon. She knew that Hoppy Jackson was not far away, wrapped in his own tarp and blanket, but able to see where she was at all times. Now, with this tall, good-looking man nearby, she felt secure and unafraid.

She slept, her lips curled in a slight smile, her last thoughts upon the kiss he had given her.

As for Blue, he was deeply stirred. He had known women of various natures during his lifetime, but this was the first time there had been such a surge within him, a surge to protect, to respect and yes, the thought struck through his mind, to love!

He did not seek his blankets, but saddling his horse, he relieved one of the men from riding herd and joined another, circling the animals, singing softly and wondering what the future held for him and for Ellen Turner.

* * *

The roundup was completed. He and another hand compared notes and, with their tally, he sought out Ellen Turner.

'How many critters did you think you had?' he asked.

She thought for a moment. 'We lost around three hundred head to the rustlers, which were never recovered. Counting range attrition, loss to wolves, such things, I would think there should be around twelve hundred head.'

He shook his head. 'You've lost another hundred head or so, over and above those originally stolen. We counted a thousand seventy head.'

She was crestfallen. 'Where would that many disappear to?' She looked at Blue. 'Do you know the country well enough now, to search for them? They surely haven't been shipped. Someone would have seen and surely would have told me.'

Blue looked at Noah who had ridden up and heard Ellen's question.

'Miss Ellen, I think I know the range about here pretty well. I'd be obliged if you'll let me go with him.'

She hesitated. 'Is your leg healed enough for such rough work? I wouldn't want you further injured on my account.'

He nodded and grinned, 'I'm about as good as I'll ever be, Miss Ellen. I'd be mighty proud to help Blue find them critters.'

'If they are to be found,' she murmured. Then nodded. 'After we get the cattle spread out again, and closer to the headquarters than before, you two make it your priority to find those cattle. I'm depending on you.'

She looked at Blue. 'I want three hundred rounded up and driven to the railhead next week. The bank is pushing me for payment of a loan. That will just about pay it off.'

Blue nodded. 'We'll see that it's taken care of, Miss Ellen,' he said. As he spoke she met his glance and blushed, recalling the kiss he had given her the evening before.

* * *

Two weeks later Blue watched as the ST crew drove three hundred of the heavy, short-horn cattle out of the pasture where they had been held for selection before shipment.

Ellen stood beside him at the corral and silently contemplated her holdings. Five hundred legally filed acres which contained a small creek meandering through the land, several small springs that had so far continued to be sufficient for the amount of cattle she owned. The three hundred being shipped brought her herd down to just slightly over eight hundred head. True, there were several cows showing evidence of pregnancy. The herd would grow, but it was a slow process, and the continued need of money for special foods was an ever-present concern.

Blue stood beside her, his eyes brooding on her face. He felt her frustration and wished there was something he might do to help her in her confusion.

'If it's all right with you,' he told her quietly, 'Noah and I will take two or three days and look for those stolen critters. You are the only rancher with Herefords. None has been shipped since the roundup a year ago. So they are being held somewhere. We'll find them.'

She looked at him then, her face reflecting her worry. She nodded. 'Take the time needed, Blue. With the boys gone with the herd, there's little to do about the ranch. I intend catching up with the herd and to be there at the shipment. Hoppy and one other of the men will be here at headquarters.'

* * *

Noah and Blue set out from the ranch headquarters early the morning after the herd had left, being driven to a railhead for shipment. Noah paused in saddling his horse and looked over at Blue.

'Where we goin', lookin' for them critters?' he asked, his dark face serious.

Blue was thoughtful. 'Apparently they disappeared from the pastures over near the mesa. I thought we'd look over that way for tracks. Of course, winds and rain may have wiped out most of the traces.'

Noah nodded. 'I just had a thought. You remember when we ran together at that clearing not so far from here? Well, I got shot when I topped the rim of a coulee. An' I recollect seein' some critters down that coulee which looked mightily like these of Miss Turner.'

Blue mounted and looked at Noah. 'I think we should go where we got together and backtrack where you came from. We just might find what we're looking for.'

⋆ ⋆ ⋆

Homer Ragsdale came into Fall Creek Saloon and gestured to Mel Lewis. The former ST ranch foreman stood at the bar. He brought his drink with him and sat at a table with the banker.

'You know we have not had a marshal in Fall Creek for some time. It is a need to be filled, what with strangers and travelers coming through recently. How would you like the job?'

Lewis sat his drink down, eyeing Ragsdale intently.

'Me? Town marshal?'

Ragsdale nodded. 'We need someone who is not afraid to confront the rough element that comes in. The last marshal was too old and too timid. He was shot in an alley behind the livery.'

Lewis was silent for a moment. 'Who would I be reportin' to? You or some storekeeper who's too afraid of a gun to let me use my own when it is necessary?'

'You will report directly to me. I will handle the town council. Say you will take the job and I'll have the star on your vest by tomorrow morning.'

Lewis sipped his drink, his thoughts roaming. It centred on Blue, who had shouldered him out of a job on the ST spread. It would be a great satisfaction to see Blue and maybe even that darkie, Noah, behind bars. He nodded.

'I'll take the job,' he said.

7

Blue and Noah entered the clearing where they had first met. They paused, looked around and Noah nodded.

'This is the place,' he said. He pointed. 'I come out of them bushes right there, an' saw you on your hoss. I guess I just lost it all then, for I don't remember much until I come to in the bunkhouse.'

Blue looked about. 'This is it,' he agreed. 'You came out of the bushes there, looking like you was almost a white man with your pain.'

Noah looked about. 'What is your plan?' he asked.

Blue was thoughtful. 'Well, I am not the best tracker in the world. But maybe, with both of us working on it, we will be able to backtrack you and find the coulee where you were shot.'

He reined his horse into the brush:

mesquite, scrub oak and a few pines. Noah followed closely, both of them eyeing the ground carefully. Blue pulled up and pointed.

'There are tracks, coning into the clearing. I suspect they are yours, since none of our crew has been over this area.'

Moving slowly, carefully scrutinizing the ground, they followed the tracks. It was erratic, Noah having been wounded badly and barely capable of hanging onto his saddle. Following the wandering passage of the horse through the brush was time-consuming. It was almost noon when Noah reined in his horse. Blue did the same, looking at his companion.

'Listen,' Noah said softly. 'I thought I heard a cow bawl.'

Blue quieted his horse and they sat listening. It was faint, but they could hear the sound of cattle grunting and now and then raising their voices, which carried beyond wherever they were corralled.

'I thought I saw some critters around here, just before I was made a target,' Noah murmured. He lifted the reins from the saddle horn where he had dropped them. 'Right over there,' he pointed. 'The wind's comin' from that direction.'

Blue nodded. 'You are a pretty good tracker, after all.' He grinned at his dark partner. 'Let's find those critters, and see if they just might belong with their brothers and sisters back on the ST spread.'

It did not take them long. With the tracks of Noah's earlier movement through the area, leaving tracks and broken brush as signs, they approached a slight lift in the land, and the dark cowboy pulled up.

'I think I was on that rise there,' he said softly. 'I sat on my hoss there an' was wondering what such fine beef was penned up for in such a place, then someone began shootin' at me. Before I could get my hoss turned, I was hit.'

They dismounted, tethered their

horses to a small scrub pine and approached the lip of the rise. Crouching behind brush cover, they raised their heads and peered over the rim of the coulee.

There was a small herd of Herefords enclosed within the coulee, which opened into a clearing, with a small stream running through it. Blue swept the space with a quick glance and immediately saw that the animals were guarded by three men.

The entrance to the coulee was narrow, and one man sat on a small boulder just inside the opening, guarding against any approach from that position. Two other men lounged about a small fire, smoking and talking. All three men were armed with sixguns on their hips, the guard at the entrance to the coulee held a rifle across his lap, and there were two rifles leaning against a saddle near the fire. Hobbled on a small flat, several feet from the fire, were their horses.

Blue eased back away from the bush,

and joined Noah, kneeling, his rifle poised, his eyes continuing to move around the area.

'I count about three hundred cattle. They are all Herefords. And Miss Ellen is the only rancher in this neck of the woods that runs such cattle.'

Noah nodded. 'They're hers, all right. An' you know something else?'

Blue looked at him questioningly. 'What?'

'This ain't on the ST land, Blue. This is N slash W land, an' I suspect Mr Wolfgang knows all about it.'

Blue was thoughtful. 'I wonder. But right now, I'm thinking how we can get the ST critters away from these three jaspers and haze them back where they belong.' They settled back of the bushes and Blue considered their problem thoughtfully. Finally he nodded and looked at Noah.

'We might be wise just to walk away from this, and turn it over to the sheriff. But before he could get here, they would have the cattle out and shipped

— think, my friend, we have to do something about it ourselves.'

Noah looked at him and then nodded slowly. 'They's only three of them an' we can surprise them. That'll take out one of them, at least. I think we could handle the other two.'

Blue looked at him. 'Noah, you got it right. Tell you what I think. We get our horses, rush in there. I'll take the guard with the rifle. You put the other two under your gun. That should do it. We'll take their guns, tie then up and haze the critters back where they belong. By the time they get loose, we'll be on ST land.'

Noah rose slowly and walked toward their waiting horses. 'No time like the present, Mr Blue. Time's awastin'.'

They eased out of their hiding place, circled, then paused a few yards from the entrance to the coulee.

Blue eased his sixgun in the leather, and taking his rifle in one hand, looked at his companion.

'You got your rifle ready?' he asked.

Noah silently reached down and pulled a twelve-gauge shotgun from a saddle sheath. 'Ain't got no rifle,' he said. 'But me an' old Betsey here will get the job done.'

Blue nodded grimly. 'Then, let's do it!'

Blue settled in the saddle and then, giving his horse an unaccustomed jab with the blunt spurs, entered the coulee with a yell.

'Yaa — eee.' The old Confederate army yell came easily to his lips. Noah, right behind him, echoed the scream.

The entrance guard leaped to his feet, staring at the two horsemen bearing down upon him and swung the rifle about for a shot. Blue's rifle shifted and spat flame and smoke and the guard tumbled to the ground, falling upon his rifle.

The two men about the fire whirled and dived for their rifles as Noah's horse scattered the coals and ashes of the camp-fire. The dark cowboy pulled up his mount and, as the two men turned, leveled the shotgun at them.

'Now . . . now,' he said. 'You boys just lay them rifle guns down and raise your hands, or you'll be joinin' your friend, wherever he went.'

Cornered, the yawning bore of the big shotgun trained on them, the two men raised their hands. One of them hesitated as his hand brushed his sixgun-butt, but the ominous click of the shotgun hammer being eared back, brought his arms well above his head.

Blue rode up and looked at the two men. 'You rannies belong to the Wolfgang spread?' he asked, eyeing them coldly.

One of them swallowed quickly with dry throat and then shook his head vigorously.

'Nope. We ain't workin' fer the N slash W spread.'

Noah wiggled his shotgun. 'I'll just bet you are bustin' to tell Mr Blue here, just who you work fer an' who was goin' to take these critters penned up here, out of yer hands.'

The two men stood sullenly and refused to talk, looking defiantly at Blue. One of them shook his head.

'Nope. We don't sell out them that pays us wages fer what we do.'

'Even to rustling cattle?' Blue's voice snapped like a whip. 'Men in these parts are hung for just what you are doing here. Getting ready to sell stolen cattle.'

One of the men started and jerked a look at his companion. 'I ain't no cow-thief,' he muttered. 'I was just doin' a job and bein' paid good fer doin' it.' He stared up at Blue who sat on his horse, his rifle trained upon them.

'I ain't goin' to be hung fer a rustler.' He gestured a thumb at the bunched cattle further down in the coulee. 'Feller by the name of Lewis hired us to just keep these critters penned up until he told us to drive them somewhere he said.'

'Lewis? Mel Lewis?' Blue asked.

The man nodded his head. 'Yeah,

him. He said these critters was his an' he could prove it.'

Noah shook his head. 'He was usin' you for a rustlin' drive. We caught you.' He turned to Blue. 'Now I guess there's only to see that they get hung for what he ordered them to do.'

Blue nodded gravely. 'That's the way I see it.'

At last the other man spoke. 'I agree with Smitty here. We don't want no trouble.' He looked at Blue a moment. 'Can we work a deal with you?'

Blue eyed him silently. There was considerable doubt in his mind that either of them could be trusted. However, more hands were needed to take this many cattle out of the coulee and drive them to meadows on the ST land. He mused this aloud to Noah.

'We can take these rannies into Fall Creek and hold them in the jail there, and wire the sheriff to come get them.' He looked silently at the two rustlers for another long minute. 'We can take them back to the N slash W headquarters and let Nathan Wolfgang hang them, since they used his land here in committing a crime.' He was silent again, his face serious. Noah nodded, considering Blue's surmising.

'Or you two, rustlers or not, can help us get these critters back where they belong. You will be free then, to go wherever you want, so long as it is where I never meet up with you again. If that would happen, I would shoot you on sight. My deal. Help us drive the cattle back to the ST pastures, and you can leave. Leave this area and never come back. That's the deal.'

Noah nodded again. 'Sounds right kindly to me, Mr Blue. How about you two?' he asked the two captured rustlers.

They eyed each other, one moving restlessly from one foot to the other. Seeing their hesitation, Blue continued:

'Or we can tie them up, Noah,' he said to the dark rider, 'and put them there beside their dead buddy. Then we just roust the cattle out through the head of the coulee, right over them. Kinda hurtful.' He shook his head seriously. 'But that would be a quick way of getting rid of them.'

The two rustlers looked at each other. Finally one shrugged. 'I expected to die sometime, but not under the hoofs of a stampede. I guess you've got a deal, so far as I am concerned.' He looked at Blue with raised eyebrows. 'You won't shoot us when the drive's done?'

Blue shook his head. 'We unload your guns and give them back to you. When we've got the cattle where we want them, you are free to go. Just don't ever come back around here.' He gestured toward the body of their companion, lying at the entrance of the coulee.

'You two bury your friend, while Noah and I round up the cattle. Don't try to run, we'll run you down and that'll be all for you.'

The men nodded sullenly and walked to the body of their guard. They carried him to a cut bank where the lip of coulee had eroded in some flood long past and, placing him there, caved the bank down over him. By the time they had finished, Noah and Blue had the cattle beginning to head out of the coulee. The two men mounted their horses, minus guns, and reluctantly joined them.

A mile away Mel Lewis, hidden by the bole of a large pine, watched them through a pair of field-glasses, reminiscent of the late War Between the States. He gritted his teeth in frustration as he saw the cattle moving out, once again in the possession of the ST men.

8

Wild Bill Culburn sat across from Mel Lewis in the Fall Creek Saloon. A tall, slim man, approaching his forties, he looked out upon the world with frosty gaze and thin-lipped visage. Two sixguns were strapped to his thighs; they were always tied down, in gunman fashion. He eyed the marshal of Fall Creek silently, as though seeking some reason he had been called here to this small, out of the way town, on the edge of the Black Hills.

'I asked you to come here,' Lewis was saying, 'to take care of a situation that has occurred. A gunslick has come into the area and is touting the development of a cattle-raiser, who is experimenting with beef that will ruin the cattle business. I want you to take him out of our hair, scare him off or, if necessary, meet him face to face and take him out of the picture. I'll pick his place in Boot Hill whenever you say.'

The man was silent for another minute, sipping now and then from a mug of Higgens' beer, served by a curious bartender. When he would have lingered near to listen in on the conversation of the marshal and the stranger, Lewis curtly motioned him away.

At last the thin lips of the stranger moved. 'Just who is it that has got into your sugar-bowl here and you want swatted?'

Lewis eyed his table companion. 'His name is Blue. That's all.'

Wild Bill's eyes blinked. 'Blue? Did you say Blue?'

The marshal nodded. 'Yep. An' that's all of a name he has ever gave here about. He's . . . ' Lewis swallowed hard, seeming to strangle on the words . . . 'he's foreman of the ST ranch that runs them new kind of beef I was telling you 'bout.'

Culburn leaned forward, his eyes

burning into Lewis's face. 'There was a man called Blue, just that, Blue, who was involved in the cattle and sheep war of New Mexico territory a while back. He was a shootist. Killed several men before he finally ran, just ahead of federal marshals and a crowd that was howlin' to hang him.'

Lewis swallowed the lump in his throat. 'A shootist? Blue is a gunslick?'

Culburn nodded. 'He's about the best. Some say he was taught his draw by Luke Short. An' ever'one knows Short was one of the best. He ain't the fastest gun, but he takes his time, pulls his guns, aims and hits whatever he shoots at, with the first bullet.'

The marshal leaned back in his chair. He looked into the face of the man across the table from him.

'Can you take him?'

The stranger was silent. He nodded. 'At the right time and place, I can take him. But I have to pick that time and place. And,' he drilled Lewis with a steely gaze, 'I don't come cheap.'

* * *

Blue was lying on his bunk. Supper was over and the rest of the crew at personal business, repairing saddle leather, braiding lariats and smoking quietly and reading weeks-old newspapers and magazines.

Ellen Turner had returned to the ranch, satisfied with the deal she had made for the three hundred cattle she had shipped. She had received her requested amount for the cattle and was contemplating a trip into town to visit the banker, Homer Ragsdale. She had called Blue into her office, a small room just off the main entrance of the house.

'I want you to go with me,' she had concluded her report to him. 'I want you there when I lay off a large part of the loan Dad left with the ranch. And I want to rub it in that I have enough money left over to pay for the special feed I need. I won't need his loan.'

Blue nodded. 'Reckon I can side you,

Miss Ellen,' he had said, his eyes searching her face. That was the first time they had been alone together since the evening when they had kissed at the close of the roundup. However, it was far from the last time he had thought about it, the sweetness of her lips, the soft pressure of her body against him. She seemed to sense his thoughts and, as she returned his look, her face coloured and she dropped her eyes to the papers before her.

They would go into Fall Creek the next day and make payment on the loan, visit the mercantile and make the feed orders. There would be time for him to visit the saloon and have a beer. But more than that, they would be together again, and at times beyond the sight of others.

There was something on his mind that was bothering him. He recalled a hoof-track he had seen. He searched his mind for the location and the time. As he was falling asleep, he remembered. He had seen the track in mud inside the coulee where they had found the ST rustled cattle. The hoofprint indicated a cracked shoe on a hind foot. And it occurred to him as he drifted into sleep, that he had seen it before . . . somewhere.

* * *

Homer Ragsdale looked thoughtfully across his desk at the young, female owner of the ST spread. Before him was a check from a well-known and affluent slaughterhouse in Bismarck. They represented a greater business in Chicago. There was no basis for him to refuse the check. It was good. And he cursed within himself, for this was not the way he had planned. Pressure on this young owner, making her return to him again and again for money, which at a certain point would lead him reluctantly, so far as the community was concerned, to take over control and finally ownership of the ST spread. This check before him threw a big monkey-wrench into his plans. He raised his eyes and looked at Ellen Turner. He ignored the foreman, Blue, who stood against the wall beside the door, taking in the conversation and noting Ragsdale's obvious chagrin.

'This, ah, this is wonderful, Miss Turner. And you want to apply it all on your father's debt? And then borrow enough from the bank to pay for special feed, I assume.'

Ellen shook her head slowly, her eyes never leaving his face. 'No, Mr Ragsdale. I will make the final payment on the outstanding loan my father left on the ranch. And I have enough to purchase the cattle-feed needed at this time.' She nodded at the check before him. 'I assume that amount will clear the loan, with some remaining for my needs.'

Ragsdale cleared his throat. This was not the way the scene was to have been played out to his satisfaction. He tapped the desk-top with his fingers, then glanced at Blue, who stood beside the office door, his eyes cool upon the face of the banker.

'Well, ah, I'm not certain this completely clears your father's obligation to the bank. However, I will go over the books carefully and let you know within a few days.'

'We'll be in town all day.' Blue's slow drawl reached across the room to him. 'We'll be leaving about four o'clock. We'll be back for your answer at that time.' His steely gaze burned into Ragsdale's face. 'I'd suggest you have the books ready by that time, with a positive answer.'

The banker's faced reddened. He reared back in his chair, as if to blast Blue with a stinging retort. He saw Blue's frown and suddenly realized this was a situation that might turn sour on him. He nodded, relaxing.

'That, ah, that will be fine. I'll check the books and paperwork and I'm certain the loan will be cleared.'

Ellen rose, gravely nodding to the banker.

'Thank you, Mr Ragsdale. I was

certain you would do everything in your power to help us out.' She turned and, glancing at Blue with a smile in her eyes, left the room, followed by her foreman.

Ragsdale sat a long time at his desk. Finally he called a clerk and gave him the order to bring the ST ranch books up to date and to draw up a paper finalizing the loan. This done, he rose, took his hat and leaving the bank, walked hurriedly to the livery.

'Hank.' He roused the liveryman from a doze. The one-time cowboy, now retired due to a broken hip while breaking in a wild cayuse, eyed him with bleary eye. The remains of a whiskey bottle beside his stool attested to his physical and mental prowess at that moment.

'Hank, wake up. Find someone and send them out to the N slash W spread with a message to Nathan Wolfgang. I want to see him in my office no later than tomorrow morning. There's business I need to talk over with him.'

He handed Hank a dollar. 'There, that'll pay for your time and get you another bottle, as well.'

'I don't know who — '

'Find someone,' Ragsdale snapped. 'Get off your butt and find someone, now, and get them on the way to the N slash W spread.'

* * *

It was past four o'clock. Ellen and Blue had taken care of the business with the banker. Ellen carried in her saddlebag a signed and stamped copy of a statement declaring the ST ranch free and clear of indebtedness to the bank. They were a mile clear of the town limits, when Blue suddenly drew up his horse. Ellen Turner reined in her mount as well.

'Why are we stopping?' she asked, looking at Blue and then glancing around her. She gasped and stiffened in the saddle.

Two men stood in the road ahead of them. One stood in the center of the road, the other off to one side. Blue knew them immediately. They were the two rannies who had been guarding the ST rustled herd and whom Blue had forced to help round them up and take them to ST pastures. Now they were here, and apparently had made no effort to leave the area, as Blue had advised them.

'Well, Mr Blue, or whatever you call yourself,' one of them called out. 'We decided to get even with you for us losing a good job and for the way you forced us, at gun point, to work for you. I reckon it's our turn to give the orders now.'

Blue eyed them carefully. Apparently they had gone back to the coulee and recovered their weapons, for each was armed with sixgun on a thigh, and there was a rifle in a scabbard on the saddle of the one who had addressed them.

'You two are in enough trouble, as it is,' Blue said quietly. 'But, if you want a showdown, then let Miss Turner ride out of the way. No need of her getting hurt for something she was not responsible for.'

The second man, at the side of the road, moved even more along the berm. They were boxing Blue in, putting him between them for a final shootout.

'Aw, we don't want to hurt no female,' he said. 'Move your hoss out of the way, miss, an' you won't be hurt. It's the man there we're interested in.'

Ellen raised her chin and stared at him. 'I am not moving an inch,' she said firmly. 'You two men are asking for more trouble than you can imagine. Now, just stand aside and let us go our way.'

The man in the center of the road shook his head. 'Then so be it.' He narrowed his eyes, a muscle in his cheek twitched. Suddenly his hand swept down to his gun-butt.

Blue rolled from his saddle, drawing as he fell. Landing on his knees, his horse shying away, he sprawled full length and thumbed a shot at the man who had started the fight. His opponent's gun was out and blasting, flinging dirt and gravel into his face. Blue rolled quickly and thumbed another bullet and the man in the center of the road jerked, then staggered back, as blood gouted from his chest where Blue's slug had chewed its way through flesh and bone.

Ellen's horse reared and then, of its own volition, leaped away from the road, Blue's horse following it. She pulled her horse to a halt and watched with horrified eyes the final outcome of the fire-fight.

The man on the berm of the road, nearest Blue, had drawn his weapon and was firing erratically at Blue, who was rolling into a ditch beside the road. Righting himself, Blue fired at the second man and a blue hole appeared in his forehead. His pistol slipped from his fingers and he fell, twitching out the last of his life.

Blue remained still for several moments. Both of the men were down. Blue was certain one was dead, but the man in the center of the road might still be alive. Finally Blue crouched and moved over to him and nudged him. He moved slackly and Blue knew he was no longer a danger. Blue rose and standing over the body punched the empties from his pistol.

Ellen leaped from her horse and flung herself across the road and into Blue's arms. She threw her arms about him and held him tightly, pressing her head against his chest. Her body shook with her sobs and it was several minutes before she could compose herself.

Blue held her close to him and let her ride out her fear and weeping. He lowered his face against her hair and kissed her softly. At last she drew away from him and looked up into his face.

'I thought you were going to be killed,' she murmured brokenly. 'I . . . I could not stand it if I lost you now. Do you hear what I am saying?'

He nodded. 'I love you, too, Ellen Turner. For the first time in my life I am able to say that. But,' he glanced down at the two inert bodies, thrown there by the force of his bullets, 'let's get away from here. I'll send some of the boys out and have the bodies taken into town. Doc Buttler will do the rest.'

'Oh, Blue! I was so frightened. Who were they? Why were they waiting for us?'

He walked her over to her horse and helped her in mounting. He pulled his own horse about to stand beside hers, mounted and looked at her.

'They were two men who had been guarding your cattle in a draw after they had been rustled. Noah and I took the cattle away from them and I told them to get out of the country. I guess they decided to get even.'

She shuddered and gigged her horse into movement.

'Let's get home,' she said. 'This is just a little too much for me to comprehend immediately.'

He nodded and gigged his horse to keep pace with hers and they left the scene of violence.

* * *

Mel Lewis dismounted and tied his horse to a tree-limb. He moved slowly up to the lip of a small canyon and looked over. He smiled to himself and nodded. It was there, all right.

He looked about and saw no one who might be observing his movements. He slid down the canyon wall, righted himself and climbed the further wall, onto a shelf that flattened out for a hundred yards or more. It was at least fifty feet deep and he stood looking at what he had been seeking for several weeks.

A mine shaft. Piled about was some timber, greyed with the elements and age, obviously used in shoring up the mine to protect against falling rocks and debris while it was being worked. A rusted tin pan lay near his feet and he nodded knowingly. Someone had been panning the gravel of the small stream flowing through the canyon. And to one side of the entrance to the mine was a huge pile of rocks, mined and carried out and undoubtedly examined for gold.

He had heard it was here and he had searched until he had found it. Riches might be right at his feet.

It was on Ellen Turner's land.

9

Nathan Wolfgang sat at his desk in his office at his home and stared at the wall of books in front of him. His mind, however, was not caught up with thoughts from the books, all of which he had read, some of them many times, but with a question.

What was to be done about Ellen Turner and her small spread of a mere ten thousand acres, of which only five hundred were homesteaded and proven-up according to territorial laws?

Her land lay between his own huge spread and a narrow strip along the edge of the Black Hills. But it was his knowledge, coming from the capital, Pierre, that a railroad spur was to be built and would have its railhead at Fall Creek. If this was so, and he believed his source, then the ST ranch lay between himself and a fortune. Those owning land adjacent to the railroad would have a windfall and certain privileges which would give them power in the territory, monetarily and politically.

But one young woman, tinkering with livestock, stood in his way. My God! he thought. She only ran about a thousand head, cattle and horses, and here he sat with over eight thousand head! He ran a crew of a dozen men, and at roundup time, even more. What crew did she have? Four men and an elderly, worn-out cowboy as ranch cook. And she stood in his way to millions?

It was time he and the banker, Homer Ragsdale, got their heads together and came up with something which would get that penny-ante outfit out of the way.

He sighed and leaned back in his chair. Nathan Wolfgang had visions. He dreamed of power, starting here and going . . . far beyond anything he had ever thought to achieve. It was his for the taking, and Nathan Wolfgang had in the past let nothing stand in his way. He nodded, agreeing mentally with his own summary.

The ST ranch had to go and the land become his to control.

* * *

Mel Lewis sat in the banker's office and jiggled a small sack in the palm of one hand.

'I think the mine is pretty rich,' he said. 'Of course, I'm no assessor. But we could take these rocks to one at the capital and find out just how rich it looks. Goin' that far away, no one here in Fall Creek would ever know about the gold, until we let it out.'

Ragsdale listened without comment. He reached out finally and gestured for the sack. Lewis tossed it onto his palm and leaned back, a gloating look on his face.

'If it's good, then you an' me are goin' to be rich as all get out. When do you want me to take you out to the mine?'

Ragsdale did not answer. He opened the small bag and poured several small rocks into the palm of his hand. He fingered them gently and then held one of them up so the light might shine upon it. He saw the glitter, the sparks of light picked up by the stone. His heart skipped a beat. It was true! The old mine still held treasure to be had by the right person.

He carefully replaced the stones in the bag and handed them to Lewis.

'Don't trust this to anyone else,' he instructed. 'Go yourself to Pierre, have them assayed and then get back here. We'll take it from there and decide what to do when we know just how rich the mine is.'

Lewis swallowed hard then nodded. 'I'll catch the first stage out tomorrow. It's due about noon.'

Ragsdale watched as the marshal of the town pocketed the bag of stones and left his office. I'm going to have to handle Lewis carefully, Ragdale mused. There's too much, if it's good, to be saddled with a partner such as Lewis.

There was a sound of hoofs in the main street, and the bank's front door opened. Ragsdale rose from his desk and stood in the doorway of his office, watching as Nathan Wolfgang made his way across the room.

'Howdy, Homer,' Ragsdale's voice was quiet. Nathan Wolfgang did not spend his time foolishly, he knew. The owner of the N slash W spread had something in mind, other than regular banking business.

He held the office door open.

'Good morning, Nathan. Come on in.'

* * *

Blue was restless. There was something afoot that was adding up to trouble for the ST spread, and he could not get a hold on it. He recalled the hoofprint he had seen at the coulee where the ST cattle had been held. He had seen it again at the livery in Fall Creek. It was imprinted on his mind and he could not think but that it held a key to troubles which had come to Ellen Turner's ranch.

One morning, when the crew was out working the cattle, checking brakes for mommy cows who would hide there to have their young, busy at other duties needing attention on the ranch, he saddled his horse and rode to the area where Ellen had told him the body of her father had been found, killed by a bullet in his back.

Blue dismounted, tethered his horse and began to walk slowly about the area, intent upon any sign, anything that might give him a clue to the murder of Silas Turner, to the rustling of the cattle, and . . . whatever might solve some of the problems that had visited themselves upon the ranch.

A small stream wound an erratic path through a small draw, close to the place where Hoppy Jackson had indicated the body had been found. He scouted one side of the stream, waded across a narrow part, and proceeded to scout the other side, adjacent to the place where Turner had been killed. After an hour of searching, he decided his idea was empty; nothing had turned up. He left the stream and began climbing the slope leading down into the small draw. He stopped suddenly at what his eyes had registered. A hoof print!

Bending, he carefully brushed away some leaves and dried grass. His eyes narrowed. It was the hoof print he had seen near the coulee, and in the livery in Falls Creek. Carefully he brushed some more small grass stems aside. The alignment was the same; the line behind one caulk showing a small break in the metal of the shoe. This rider had been present when Silas Turner was murdered — or was the murderer!

Blue straightened, his face bleak. One man in the community was both rustler and murderer. His mind searched for clues as to the identity of such person.

But he could come up with no one. True, Mel Lewis was a character whose activities were questionable. Sam Fletcher, foreman of the N slash W spread came to mind. Nathan Wolfgang had tried to buy out Ellen Turner. These and others were considered and rejected. Some stranger was working against the ST ranch, attempting to drive it from the area, and was willing to kill and rustle stock to achieve an end. He shook his head.

He mounted and looked at the sun, judging the time. It was nearing noon. Old Hoppy Jackson had been around ever since the ST had been established. He had come into the country with Silas Turner and had worked the range with him until being injured by the wild horse. Perhaps he might have seen the track and thought nothing of it. Or, the thought came to him suddenly, there was a blacksmith in Fall Creek, who regularly shod horses. He might have seen such a hoof needing a new shoe.

Looking again at the sun and gauging

its position, he reasoned it was near and just past midday. He could get into Fall Creek, talk with the smithy and be back at the ranch by dark. Clucking at his horse, he turned it in the direction of the road into the town.

Mel Lewis walked out of the Fall Creek Saloon just as Blue rode into town and to the livery. He watched as Blue entered the stables. The marshal turned back into the room and jerked his head at Wild Bill Culburn. The lean gunman rose from the table where he and Lewis had been playing a dull, time-consuming game of five-card stud.

'Blue's in the stables. He'll come out in a minute or two. It would be a good time to brace him,' Lewis suggested.

Culburn moved to the door and watched. In a few minutes Blue appeared in the livery doorway and stood talking casually with the livery-man. Culburn eyed him and then nodded to Lewis.

'It's Blue, all right. I've been wanting to come up to him for a long time. I guess this is as good a time as any.' Shifting his pair of sixguns on his hips, settling them in their leather, he pushed open the batwing doors and stepped out onto the boardwalk in front of the saloon.

'Blue,' he called. His voice carried down the street to the livery and Blue turned toward him, questioningly. He saw the tall, thin gunman stride into the street and take a stance. A chill ran up his back. This was a killer and he was calling him out!

10

Nathan Wolfgang's face was stiff with anger. Homer Ragsdale sat in the chair behind his desk, tense, but unwilling to accede to Wolfgang's proposal.

'Nathan,' he said, through a puff of aromatic cigar smoke, 'what you're suggesting is an outright land steal. True, the Turner spread is small, and also true, it stands in your way to a clear access to the railroad spur that may come through. Notice the word 'may'. It is not yet a done deal.'

The rancher shrugged. 'We all take chances, Homer. You when you make a loan or raise a percentage on your use of money. I when I decide to add a few acres to my holdings, or trust the running of my spread to a foreman who is out to gouge me every way he can. I gamble whenever I put my money in your bank, that you won't go under and leave me holding a worthless piece of paper. But there are times when we have to take chances. If we don't take over that little spread, keeping us from the railroad, then we miss a chance for future growth.'

Ragsdale listened soberly, his mind working quickly. Mel Lewis was to take the stage out at noon today for Pierre, the territorial capital. If the assay came back with rich color and there was a chance of somehow taking the remaining gold out of the mine, then with Nathan Wolfgang taking over the ST spread, the opportunity to sudden riches was gone. If it turned out that the gold was not there, then he would back the N slash W's take-over of the Turner spread, and make certain he made a profit out of the deal. He stirred and shook his head.

'Now is not the time,' he told the rancher. 'Let it ride for several weeks. Let's see how she gets along with her experiments with the cattle. I think she'll go broke fiddling around with nature that way. If she does, then we'll make a move. There's still time, with the railroad deal not yet firm in the capital.'

Wolfgang stared at him, then shook his head. 'I might have known that you would not have the backbone for such a move. There's times when caution must be thrown to the wind.' He rose, putting on his hat. 'We will talk again. But don't figure on waiting too long.'

* * *

'Miss Ellen.' Noah stood at the back door of the house, his hat in his hand. Ellen Turner was working in the kitchen and saw him standing there. She heard him and came to the door.

'Yes, Noah, what is it?'

'Miss Ellen, is there something back there near the edge of the mesa that someone would be interested in?'

She looked at him questioningly. 'Not that I know of? Why?'

Noah looked down and shuffled his

feet hesitantly. 'Well, I've seen hoof-prints goin' an' comin' from that direction. I follered them and they end at the edge of a small canyon. Fer as I kin see, they ain't nothin' around there much that would cause anyone to make such a trip.'

Ellen was thoughtful as she dried her hands on a towel. 'Come into the kitchen, Noah,' she gestured to the door. 'Have a cup of coffee while I think about this.'

The dark cowboy nodded and entered the kitchen. She poured a cup of coffee for him and for herself and sat at the table with him. After a few minutes of talking about what he had noticed she leaned back in her chair and looked at him.

'Noah, I agree. There must be something back there apparently that has caught someone's attention.' She leaned over and freshened both cups of coffee. 'Do you think you could take me there.' There was a sudden memory of something her father had told her while he was still alive.

Noah nodded. 'Sure, Miss Ellen. But that's mighty rough country back there.'

'We can take our time. Blue is in town today and I have time on my hands. What say we go take a look?'

Since her father's death she had not remembered what her father had mentioned until Noah had brought his question to her about the mesa.

Ellen and Noah left the ranch headquarters and immediately set out for the mesa, following a thin line of hoofprints. Noah must have a good eye for tracking, she mused, as she followed the cowboy through the back range leading slowly into the upward slope toward the mountains. The mesa, first a blue line on the horizon, began to change with higher elevation. Colors changed, and the smooth line became rough the closer they came. It had been a long time since she had been this far away from the headquarters. She was surprised at the richness of graze, and the good amount of water the small creek brought through her land.

Several hours went by before they paused at the lip of a small canyon. She eased back in the saddle and looked about as she sipped from a canteen. Noah was quiet, waiting her next word or move.

She scanned the lip of the canyon, where it seemed that the hoofprints they were following ceased. She dismounted and walked to the edge and saw the signs of someone coming or going down the slope to the bottom of the canyon. Her eyes followed the direction of the footprints and, rising above the small stream at the bottom of the canyon, rested on a flat shelf covered with boulders and a mound of rocks and debris.

It was then she recalled what it was her father had told her.

There was the dark opening of a mine. Used many years back and apparently abandoned, lost to the memory of the residents of the area, but being of interest to someone who was careful to keep her from knowing of his presence — or reasoning.

Who might it be? And — was the mine still valuable?

* * *

Tall, thin his legs spread in a stance of ready and waiting, the gunman stood in the main street of Fall Creek, his narrowed gaze upon the form of Blue, who had just emerged from the livery stables.

'Blue, I'm calling you out! I've waited a long time to face you and this is as good a time as any.'

There was a rattle and pound of wheels and racing hooves, and the stage entered the town and came to a rushing halt amid dust and jingling harness before the saloon. The driver saw the tableau of the gunman facing Blue and remained riveted to his seat. He felt his span of horses and his two passengers were out of the line of fire, and he waited the outcome of the confrontation between the two men.

Blue eyed the now straddle-legged stance of the gunman. He slowly turned sideways to the challenger, and casually slipped the leather thong from the hammer of his sixgun.

'Blue, you sided the sheepmen over the cattlemen in the Lincoln County fracas down there in New Mexican territory. I lost money and face and you turned your back and ran when the affair got too hot for you. Now, you are going to pay.'

Suddenly Blue recalled the man, his size, his shape and the occasion of an earlier confrontation with him. Wild Bill Culburn had led an unruly gang, pretending to be the spokesman for the cattle association in the quarrel over grazing rights in that area. Blue had challenged their position and faced them in what had turned out to be a routing of the gang. He left, knowing that one man or a few men would be the answer to the problem. Cooler heads would prevail and arrive at a solution for the situation. Not, however, before the end of three long years of fighting and quarreling, and the loss of lives.

'Culburn,' Blue said, his voice calm and carrying across the space between them, 'that was long ago, and settled to the satisfaction of those concerned. Our part was done and lost in the total importance of the affair. Let bygones be bygones and forget it.'

Culburn shook his head. 'Nope. I've waited a long time for this and I'm gonna get my satisfaction. I'm gonna kill you, Blue, and be satisfied for the first time in years.' He squared away, facing Blue fully. 'This is it! Go for your gun!'

Mel Lewis came from the saloon where he had been awaiting the arrival of the stage. Carrying a single valise, he stood beside the stage, one hand upon the door. He was going to see the outcome of the gunfight, but he was not, marshal or not, going to stay around for the work of the lawman for the town. The mayor could take care of it himself, or the town council who had hired him. He was on his way to the territorial capital on a business trip for Homer Ragsdale that was far more important than to see about the burial and/or jailing of a gunman, whatever the outcome.

'If that's the way it has to be,' Blue said, his eyes on those of his opponent. Luke Short, who had taught him all he knew about the use of the sixgun, had told him, 'Watch the eyes. They'll tell you when the man is going to move, every time. Watch them.'

Culburn tensed, his eyes narrowed to gleaming slits, and his right hand slashed down to his gun-butt, drawing the black steel weapon and thumbing the hammer as he did so. As the weapon cleared leather, Blue, following the actions of his opponent, seeing the narrowing of the eyes, and the flexing of the fingers above the gun-butt, drew and fired, his hand a blur of speed. As

Culburn's slug whistled past his ear, his own bullet struck the gunman in the side, boring through muscle, artery and liver.

Culburn yelled in pain and dropped his pistol, his hands grabbing his right side. Blood spread through his clothes and filled his hands. He raised his head, glaring at Blue, and then toppled into the dust of the street. He stiffened and twitched, then relaxed, quite still as death carried him into its eternal folds.

Blue grimaced and relaxed. He leaned against the stable door, slowly ejected the spent shell and replaced the load in the chamber of his Colt. His eyes brooded, looking down the street to the crowd gathering around the gunman.

* * *

Mel Lewis had seen the entire tableau erupt into violence and play out its deadly sequence. He stood beside the stage, thinking. Then he stepped back and called to the driver, who had joined the crowd around the dead body.

'Sam, you go on without me. I'll catch the next stage in the morning.'

The driver turned and looked at him and waved. ' 'Sall right, Mel,' he called back. 'I'm gonna get me a drink in the saloon and settle my nerves.' He walked over to the stage and spoke to the two passengers.

'Be about a half-hour before we leave. Might as well get out an' stretch your legs.'

Lewis sat his valise beside the saloon door, turned and walked up the street to where Blue was preparing to enter the stables. His former reason for being in town to investigate the strange hoofprint was forgotten. He saw Lewis coming and turned to face him, his face expressionless. He was certain the marshal was going to roust him about the gunfight, but the stable hand stood just beyond the door and had seen the entire event.

'Blue,' Lewis called. 'Hold up there.

Don't get your horse. You're under arrest.'

Blue faced him. The marshal stood ten feet away, his face taut, his right hand on the butt of his pistol.

'What are you charging me with?' Blue asked, his voice soft, his eyes never straying from the marshal's right hand.

'For murder. I saw you gun down this here stranger in the street. Never even give him a chance to draw.'

The livery owner moved to the doorway. 'Marshal, I saw every bit of the fracas. It was self-defence. Blue never drawed his gun until that feller there had cleared his holster.'

'You stay out of this,' Lewis snarled at the liveryman. 'I saw it all, and I saw it different. Come on, Blue, you can eat on the county until the judge gets around here on his trip through.'

11

Higgens, the bartender at the saloon in Fall Creek, removed his apron and laid it on the bar. 'Ray,' he called to one of his helpers. 'You take over and run the place for awhile. I've got something I have to do.'

Ray, a broken-down cowboy, with a game leg, placed the broom he had been using on the sawdust floor and came over to where Higgens was taking his hat from behind the bar. The barkeeper hesitated and then, reaching down again, brought out the double-barreled shotgun.

'You goin' huntin'?'

'Might be I will see a deer on the way,' Higgens said over his shoulder and shoved his way through the batwing doors and onto the street.

'Huntin' deer, with a shotgun?' Ray grunted, as he bit off a mouthful of plug tobacco. 'No way. There's something else on his mind, such as it is.'

While Higgens was on his way out of town, Mel Lewis, the marshal, was in the office of the banker, Homer Ragsdale. The rotund banker was red of face, almost stuttering in his anger, his eyes bulging at the marshal.

'You were supposed to be in that stage and on the way to the capital with that ore to be assayed. Now it will be another day until you can be on your way. You don't seem to understand how important that is to both of us.'

The marshal cringed under the onslaught, but faced up to the banker sitting across the desk from him.

'That Blue fellow killed a man on the streets of my town. I had to jail him before he got away. He's in jail now, and I appointed a deputy to take care of him until I get back.'

Ragsdale snorted. 'Lewis, I saw that fight from the door of the bank. It was clear as day that Blue defended himself. His gun cleared the holster *after* that gunnie had drawn and was bearing down on him. Several people saw it. You haven't a leg to stand on. Turn him loose, and get on with what I asked you to do.'

Lewis shook his head stubbornly. 'I didn't see it that way. I'll go to the capital, all right. But Blue stays in jail, at least until I can get back and question a few others who saw the fight.' He rose and slapped his hat on his head. 'Don't be so high and mighty with me, Ragsdale. We are in this thing together, don't you ever forget that!' He left the room slamming the office door behind him.

⋆ ⋆ ⋆

Higgens had never been to the ST ranch, but he knew the direction and by mid-afternoon was hitching his horse to the corral nearest the house. Hoppy Jackson came to the door of the bunkhouse and called to him.

'You're kinda off your regular diggin's, ain't you, Higgens?'

The bartender paused and nodded. 'Howdy, Hoppy. Yeah, I'm stickin' my nose into something that may not be any of my business, but I thought you'd need to know.'

'Know what?' Ellen Turner had come from the house and stood on the porch, looking down at Higgens.

'Miss Ellen,' the bartender removed his hat and held it nervously before him. 'I ain't one to carry tales, but I thought I would make an exception this time. That Blue feller, your foreman, I guess, is in deep trouble.'

Ellen came down off the porch and stood before him, her eyes questioning him. 'What kind of trouble, Higgens?'

'Marshal Lewis put him in jail this morning. Blue was in a gunfight with some stranger in town. Blue downed the feller but the marshal put him in jail.'

Hoppy had left the bunkhouse and was standing close by, listening to the bartender. He snorted.

'Well, for one, I saw it all and know that Blue was last to draw his gun and that the stranger fired the first shot. He missed an' Blue didn't. An' Blue fired, a second or two after the stranger.'

'Then Blue was jailed by the marshal? After it was said that Blue was not the cause of the fight?' Ellen asked.

Higgens nodded. 'That's right. An' Lewis has left town now, an' there's a deputy watchin' Blue.'

'How long will the marshal be gone?' asked Hoppy.

Higgens shook his head. 'It's two days by stage to the capital, an' two days back. Then count the time it takes for him to do whatever he's goin' there for. Five days, at least, maybe more.'

Ellen turned to Hoppy. 'Go find Noah, and get two other of the boys. I think it's time we paid a visit to town.'

* * *

Nathan Wolfgang paced his office. It was a spacious room in a large, well-appointed house. Books lined the shelves, and the desk and chairs were of finest material, ordered out and shipped in from Chicago. Nathan's wife had been dead many years. As he grew more affluent, he pleased himself by arranging the world about him to his advantage, which included his home. He was well read, grasping and willing to go to any length to achieve a purpose or a desire. Right now, as he paced, he planned how he *must* acquire the small ranch of Ellen Turner, which stood between himself and the possibility of untold riches. This was dependent upon the railroad coming through along the reef of the mesa and into Fall Creek as a railhead for cattle shipment from the ranches in the surrounding territory.

* * *

Homer Ragsdale was worried. Ever since Mel Lewis had found the old mine on the back of the ST range, and they saw there was the possibility of mining it for further rich ore, he had worried about Nathan Wolfgang and what he might do toward acquirement of the ST ranch, thus cutting access to the mine. And Lewis was at least five days away on the trip to the capital to procure an assay of ore from the mine.

He was restless. Several people had come to him and stated that Blue, the ST foreman, had been wrongly jailed, that he had been the second to draw his gun in the recent fracas, and that he had, in fact, fired after being fired upon. This was going to cause problems with the owner of the ST ranch, and at the present Ragsdale wished nothing to cause her further disturbance. He had plans to purchase her holdings, reasoning with her that the experimentation with a new breed of cattle was a lost cause. He hoped to at least lease her holdings until such time as he and Lewis might strip the mine of any remaining riches, given that the assay was positive.

He sighed. Things were not falling

into place as he wished. Too many variables, and Nathan Wolfgang was one of the uppermost. He decided a talk with Wolfgang was necessary. Cool him down and persuade him to hold back from any immediate plan to take over the ST ranch.

* * *

It was midnight. There was no moon. There was a light here and there from a window. But along the few streets of the town, there was no movement until four horsemen moved from the shadows of the trail that led into town. They paused and sat observing the main street.

As one they moved down the street and paused before the town jail, each pulling up at the hitch rail in front of the building. Three of them dismounted and handed their reins to the fourth, who remained mounted.

One of them tried the door and found that it was locked from the inside. While two moved up beside the door, the man knocked again and again.

Wally Hubbard, the appointed deputy, was asleep on a cot in the office. There was only one occupant in the cells. Blue awoke at the first knock and stood beside his cell door, alert to whatsoever was taking place.

Hubbard awoke, grunting, rolled out of his blankets and took up his sixgun from the desk. He moved to the door.

'Who is it an' what d'you want?'

'There's been a bank robbery,' a voice told him. 'And they are coming out of the bank right now with a sack of money. You'd better get out there and stop them.'

Hubbard was no hero. Neither was he unusually brainy. He moved slow and thought as slowly. But the word robbery caught in his mind and he unlatched the door and held it open.

'Who — ' he began and that was the last word he spoke for several hours. A gun-butt slapped his temple and he collapsed across his cot. The three shadows moved into the jail and closed the door behind of them.

'The keys are in the top desk-drawer,' Blue said. One of the men laughed and Blue recognized Hoppy Jackson's voice.

In a minute they found the keys and Hoppy unlocked the cell and opened it. Blue stepped out and Noah moved up and handed him his belt and sixgun.

'You do find the most unusual places to spend the night,' the dark cowboy drawled. Blue chuckled.

'Believe me,' he said, 'it was not my choice. But let's get out of here.' He paused at the cot and looked down at Hubbard. He reached down and placed fingers at the man's throat and felt the beat of his pulse. 'The deputy will live,' he murmured. 'He may have a sore head for a few days. Come on, Let's vacate.'

Outside the building he paused and looked up at the girl holding the horses. 'Miss Ellen, you do turn up in the most unusual places and at unusual times.'

He grinned up at her, his teeth gleaming white in the darkness.

'It's my nature to do so,' she murmured to him. 'If you are ready, the horse on the right is yours.'

In a moment Blue was mounted and the group of now five moved down the street and onto the trail out of town.

Blue rode beside Ellen Turner and reaching out he touched her hand. She looked at him seriously, squeezed his hand and then moved on.

Behind them the town was quiet. No one had seen or heard them and Wally Hubbard would never know for sure who it was that had robbed the jail of its single occupant.

* * *

Nathan Wolfgang had made up his mind. Regardless of the hesitation of Homer Ragsdale, it was time to move. If the railroad was coming through the range over which the ST ranch had control, then he and other ranchers in the territory would suffer.

It was time to move. With this in mind, he called in his foreman, Sam Fletcher, and began to make plans for the takeover of the ST ranch.

12

Ellen Turner heard the sound of hoofs coming into the yards beside the barns and sheds. It sounded as though there were several riders and she left what she was doing in her office and moved to the front door. of the house. Her eyes widened when she saw the large group of cowboys. Sam Fletcher, the N slash W outfit's foreman, and leading them the small, straight, stern-faced Nathan Wolfgang.

Wolfgang and the foreman left the group and rode to the front of the house. Ellen stepped out upon the porch and faced them, her eyes questioning.

'Miss Turner.' Wolfgang spoke in his whining voice, leaning toward her, his eyes hot upon her face.

'Mr Wolfgang, to what do I owe this sudden visit? And with so many riders?'

'I am taking possession of your holdings, Miss Turner,' Wolfgang rasped. 'I will give you an honest price for your land and for your buildings. I will sell off the cattle you have branded. The unbranded will henceforth carry the N slash W brand.'

She paled. 'You cannot do this! This ranch is mine, willed to me by my father. I have cared for it and improved upon it. There is no price you can offer acceptable to me. This is mine, and I do not intend selling one inch, one beef, to you.' She squared her shoulders and stared at him with anger bright in her eyes.

Wolfgang shrugged. 'There is no argument, Miss Turner. You stand in the way of future development in the territory. I speak for all the ranchers, thinking of their welfare as well as my own. You will pack a valise of what you will need for a trip to Pierre. You will be my guest tonight. Tomorrow two of my men will escort you to town and see you off on the stage. I will see that a good price for your land and holdings is deposited in the bank at Fall Creek.'

Ellen stared at him, stiff with anger and with a fear beginning to creep into her mind. This man was serious. He was taking her ranch and sending her off as though she were a beef animal for sale.

'You mean I have no say in this matter?'

He shook his head. 'None whatsoever. I work for the good of the territory and my act and words will be substantiated by others in the community.'

'I will not set foot — '

He looked at Sam Fletcher. 'Take her into the house and stuff some of her clothes in a valise, a sack, or something. Let's get on with it.'

Hoppy Jackson had come from the back of the bunkhouse when the crowd arrived. He had slipped through the main house and stood just inside the front room, listening to what was happening. When Sam Fletcher dismounted and approached Ellen, he slipped out again, and hurried to the bunkhouse. There he gathered up gear and a rifle and disappeared into a copse of piñons back of the barns.

Fletcher took hold of Ellen's arm. She jerked loose from him and slapped his face resoundingly.

'Take your hands off me! I'll do what you say, for I have no choice.'

'Where are your men?' Wolfgang suddenly looked about. No hands were in sight. There was no one standing near the bunkhouse, mess-shack or barns.

'They are doing what all honest hands do when there is work to be done. They do not go attacking lone women and seizing their ranches!' Ellen said calmly and coldly. 'Now, get this creature off my porch and I will pack a valise. But, mind you, Nathan Wolfgang, you are opening a can of worms you will regret for the rest of your life!' With that she turned and entered the house, leaving an expressionless rancher staring at her, and his foreman rubbing a reddened cheek where her hand had landed resoundingly.

* * *

Having rescued Blue from the jail, Ellen had led them to an abandoned line shack just under the rim of the mesa.

'It hasn't been used for years,' she said, 'but I'm certain you can make do until the hue and cry of your escape has died down. I haven't seen hide nor hair of you for days.'

Noah stayed with Blue, to get the shack into livable condition, and Hoppy returned to the ranch. Later he brought them blankets, canteens, ammunition for their rifles, and several bags of food.

'You can kill your own meat,' he told them. 'But don't come back to the ranch until I come and tell you.'

Hoppy was at the shack sooner than he had expected. He watched from the trees, seeing Nathan Wolfgang and his men surround Ellen Turner and ride off with her. He had heard enough of the conversation to know that Ellen Turner had been taken by Wolfgang and that she was going to be put on tomorrow's stage to Pierre. Two of Wolfgang's men would be putting her on the stage.

Losing no time, knowing there was nothing he could do, Hoppy had left the ranch and raced to the line shack where Noah and Blue were staying for the moment.

Blue came to the door of the shack when he heard the sound of hoofs. His eyes narrowed when he saw Hoppy and instantly realized something was very wrong for the cook to be in such a hurry. When Hoppy flung himself from the saddle, Blue was there to grasp the reins of his horse.

'What's up?' he asked. crisply.

'There's hell to pay,' Hoppy panted, wiping his forehead with a bandanna. 'Wolfgang's took over the ST spread and took Miss Ellen with him.'

Blue's face whitened and his jaws tightened. He had not trusted the N slash W owner to any great extent, but that he might do such a high-handed thing to a fellow rancher was far beyond the ethical code of the time. Men helped men, they did not hinder their endeavours.

'See that?' Hoppy thumbed back across his shoulder. A huge black column of smoke rose to the sky from the direction he had come.

'They set the main house an' barns afire. There was nothing I could do. So I high-tailed it for here.'

Blue nodded. He looked at Noah who had come up as Hoppy came into the shack's yard.

'Let's get some grub in us and do some thinking about what we can do for Miss Ellen,' he said grimly.

* * *

Mel Lewis was livid with anger when he returned from Pierre and found that Blue had been broken from the jail. He browbeat Wally Hubbard for allowing it to happen.

When he met with Homer Ragsdale, Lewis was taken over the coals for leaving Blue under the careless care of Hubbard. It was several minutes before the banker calmed down and with shaking hands took a cigar from his humidor and lighted it. When it was going to his satisfaction he settled back in his chair, quietened.

'Well, what's done is done. We'll face the consequences when we come to them. Now, what's the report on the mine?'

Lewis sat slowly overcoming his anger at the banker for blaming him for the loss of the ST foreman. He eyed the rotund Ragsdale across the desk, and arrogantly rolled and lighted his own cigarette. After the first deep draw, he blew out the smoke and eyed the banker through the haze.

'There's some good ore there,' he told the banker slowly, savoring the look of expectation on Ragsdale's face. 'And we can get at it without any problem.'

'How? What do you mean?' The banker leaned forward in his chair.

Enjoying the hold he had upon the banker's desire for the report, Lewis drew on the cigarette again and emitted the smoke, before answering.

'The ST line, staked and filed, is a quarter-mile shy of the mined area. It's on open land and never filed on. Whoever mined there was doing it, hoping to find a mother-lode an' scat with it, without bothering about the law. Unless Ellen Turner tries to horn in on it, we're home free.'

Ragsdale eyed Lewis quietly. He did not trust the marshal any further than he could throw a bucket of water without spilling it. Yet the man was useful. He wore the badge of town marshal because Ragsdale wished it so. He would do, within reason, whatever the banker said. Still, as Ragsdale looked at him, the banker did not trust him to reveal all he had found out about the mine.

'Is there more?'

Lewis hesitated, then nodded. 'Yeah. I filed on the land that has the mine on it.'

Ragsdale straightened in his chair. 'Filed on it? How much acreage?'

'I made a homestead filing, about half a section.'

'Then we own all the land the mine is on?'

'Yep,' Lewis grinned. 'An' I put us down as partners. We're owners of a hundred-sixty acres of land, on which is a mine that shows signs of good ore!'

* * *

The stage rolled out of Fall Creek the day following Wolfgang's seizure of the ST holdings. Ellen Turner was now dry-eyed after a long night in one of the N slash W bedrooms. She had been given a good evening meal, which she hardly touched. And flapjacks and coffee before they set out to meet the stage. Two of Wolfgang's men were with her, one sitting beside her on the poorly padded seat of the stage, the other sitting opposite her. He slouched on the seat, his hat canted down over his forehead, from under which his eyes rested on her unblinkingly. She was empty of grief, now filled with thoughts of what was going to happen to her.

'Money will be placed in the Fall Creek bank,' Nathan had told her in his whining voice. 'You can send for it after you get wherever you go. I would suggest St Louis, or Chicago. Don't stay in Pierre. That will be a mistake. If you try to cause me trouble, I'll hunt you down.'

She shuddered to think of his words and expression, so cold and mean. He had taken her ranch, her cattle and burned the buildings. She was on her way out of the territory, and there was nothing she was able to do about it.

Nathan Wolfgang paced his spacious study, smoked his cigar. He rubbed his hands together gleefully. He had done it. The woman might try to take the ranch back. But what would she have?

Buildings burned, her cattle now on his own range and she on her way out of the territory. If she tried to cause him trouble, she would learn what real trouble was!

* * *

The stage was five miles out of Fall Creek. It slowed down for a sharp bend in the road, which dipped through a steep-banked coulee. At the rim of the coulee, the horses pulling hard, the stage was at its slowest speed of the trip.

The driver pulled up and brought the stage to a halt. Three men moved quickly into the road and one of them, whom he knew, held a Sharps .50 calibre pointing at him.

'Now, Hoppy Jackson, you be right careful of that there cannon you're carryin'. What do you want with this stage? We ain't shippin' no money nor anything else worth much.'

Hoppy grinned at him. 'You've got somethin' on the stage worth more than any *thing* you might be carryin'. You jist set still and let things happen.'

Noah moved to one side of the stage and Blue to the other.

'Everyone out,' Blue said, alert to anything either of the men he saw in the stage might do. 'Miss Ellen, you come on out now. There's a horse waiting for you!'

13

The man sitting across from Ellen Turner whirled about as the stage stopped and, as Noah moved up to the side of the stage, grabbed his sixgun and burst out of the stage's door, firing as he landed on the ground.

His shots went wild, and as he slid to a halt and turned to encounter the dark rider again, Noah's double-barrelled .12 gauge shotgun roared once. The load of buckshot caught the gunman in the chest and flung him back over an embankment of the road.

The other man, seated beside Ellen Turner, started to put his arm about her, to use her as a shield, when the closed fist of the young woman struck him in the mouth. She seized his hat-brim and yanked it down over his face. As he struggled, cursing, to remove the hat, she shoved him back into the seat, seized his gun from its holster and flung the weapon out of the window. Whirling, she leaped from the door of the stage and ran to Blue.

Seeing her coming across the road to him, Blue leaped from his saddle and seized her, pushing her behind him and against his horse.

'Get behind my horse,' he told her, and turned his attention to the stage, where the second man had stepped through the door and was squaring up, to face him directly. The man threw up his hand and Blue saw the glint of steel. Ellen had thrown the man's pistol from the stage, but apparently he had a hideout, and was leveling it at Blue.

Blue's Colt .44 was in his hand. He moved it slightly and pulled the trigger as the man fired. The hideaway pistol was small, carrying a light load, not meant for distance shooting. The bullet whined past Blue and Blue's sixgun blasted. The man jerked back and collapsed against the stage, the bullet ploughing through his shoulder.

The driver of the stage yelled at Blue.

'There was just two of 'em. This one on this side is dead. That negro cowboy blasted him to Kingdom Come.'

Blue, holding his sixgun on the man, walked over and looked down at him. The man held his bleeding shoulder and cursed Blue.

'I could have drilled you centre,' Blue said coldly, 'but I want you to take a message to Nathan Wolfgang. You tell him that this fight has just begun. I'll be coming for him.'

The man glared at Blue.

'I won't carry no message for you, you killer! When I get to the next town in this stage, I'll have a federal marshal after you, as soon as I get there!'

Blue looked up at the driver and gestured to the wounded man.

'Take both of them to the next town. The marshal there can do whatever he wishes with them.'

'Whatever you say, friend.' The driver laced his lines about the brake pole and clambered down from the seat. 'One of you be kindly enough to help me load 'em?'

Noah had moved around and dismounted. 'I'll help you,' he said.

Blue turned to Ellen and took her in his arms. 'Are you all right? They didn't hurt you?' He leaned over and kissed her forehead. Unmindful of Hoppy and Noah, she wrapped her arms about his shoulders and pressed her face against his.

'They didn't hurt me,' she murmured, trembling in his arms. 'But I am afraid of what is going to happen now. I won't want you to get hurt. And it would all be my fault.'

He hugged her tightly. 'Not your fault,' he told her. 'It's the fault of a greedy man who has no conscience and is willing to do whatever he thinks necessary to have his way.' His expression changed into hard lines. 'This will be one time he won't have his way!'

The dead man and the wounded cowboy now loaded into the stage, the driver slapped his reins and yelled at the horses. They surged against the weight of the stage and then moved quickly down the road toward Pierre.

Blue led Ellen's mare, which they had brought with them, to her. He helped her into the saddle. With Hoppy and Noah leading the way, they left the road, and moved across country to the line shack where Blue and Noah had been hiding.

* * *

Noah had moved ahead of the rest and was waiting for them a mile from the shack. He motioned for them to stop as they came up to him.

'What's going on?' Blue asked, reining his horse in close to Noah so their voices would not carry.

'There's two hosses in the corral at the shack,' Noah said. 'I didn't get close enough to see brands. But there's smoke comin' out of the chimbley, like someone is cooking a meal.'

Ellen and Hoppy came up to them.

Ellen looked at Blue questioningly. 'Is there something wrong?' she asked.

Blue nodded. 'Looks like someone has moved in on our hiding-place. You and Hoppy stay back while Noah and I scout it out.'

Hoppy grimaced. 'You let me get a sight on one with this here ol' fifty an' you won't be bothered with 'em again.'

'Maybe there's no need for that,' Blue said. 'Noah and I will move up close enough we can see the brands on the horses. You two stay where you can sight me. If everything is all right I'll signal you. If not, Noah and I will start rousting them out of our nest, and then, Hoppy, we'll use your cannon, if necessary.'

Using cover of swales and clumps of bushes and trees Blue and Noah rode as close as they dared, knowing that the sound of the horses' hooves would give away their presence if they were heard. They dismounted and tethered their mounts to a tree and, carrying their long weapons moved quietly in on the shack. They centred their attention on the corral.

'That's an ST brand on one of them hosses.' Noah's keen eyes had detected the mark on the flank of one of the animals. Blue nodded and moving cautiously around, he came to where he could see the other horse. He recognized it as one of their own *remuda*. 'They are both ST horses.' He rose from his concealment and holding his rifle trained on the door of the shack he stepped out and approached the front of the building.

'Hello, the shack . . . anyone there?'

In a moment the door opened and a figure stepped out, holding a sixgun in his hand.

'Who . . . Blue? Man, we're glad to see you. We was just about ready to move on.' Another joined him, and Blue relaxed. Two of Ellen's cowhands had shown up. There had been no time to alert the hands caring for the herds when Wolfgang moved in. Blue had hoped they would sense the problem and move on, or hide out until they found where Ellen and the rest were hiding.

He turned, removed his hat and waved it to the waiting Hoppy and Ellen. 'We're glad to see you guys,' he told the men. 'Noah and Miss Ellen are on their way in.'

'Aw, we seen what was happening an' knew the place was in Wolfgang's hands. Three of the boys went on, but Rob an' me, well, we figured out this might be where you would be. If not, we'd rest a spell and then move on.'

Ellen came up and seeing the two cowboys, breathed a sigh of relief. Hoppy dismounted and went to them and shook hands.

'What are y'all burnin' in there? Smells like scorched meat to me.'

'Hoppy,' one of them said with a grin, 'we are right pleased to see you. You can take over the stove-herdin' any time you want.'

'Wa'al, I see you've learned some sense along the way since I last saw you,' Hoppy grumbled. He entered the shack to take care of whatever it was being cremated on the stove.

After a simple late afternoon meal, Blue and the men, with Ellen sitting in on the conversation, discussed their situation.

'I think it would be better if Miss Ellen did not appear too soon,' Blue told the group seriously. 'I know this isn't the best place to spend a lot of time in, but right now Nathan Wolfgang is grinding his teeth, and some of it in guilt and fear. If he were to find out she was here, he'd be on us like a coyote on a rabbit.'

Ellen nodded. 'I understand. In the meanwhile, what are we going to do, just sit here and talk about what has happened?'

Blue looked at her and shook his head slowly. 'No, ma'am,' he said softly. 'I've done some thinking on the situation and come up with one thing for sure. We've got to tweak Wolfgang's nose, and make him hurt for what he's done to Miss Ellen.' He looked around the group.

Hoppy nodded. 'Whatever it might be, it won't be enough to make up fer what he's done to her.'

The rest nodded solemnly.

'What do you have in mind, Blue?' Ellen asked. 'I hope it's not something too dangerous. I don't want any of you hurt on my account.'

'Now, Miss Ellen,' said Hoppy solemnly, 'you cain't make scrambled eggs without breakin' the shell. It may get dangerous but I expect we all will be able to make him think on his evil ways.' Again the men nodded agreement.

Blue looked at Ellen. 'I think it best if you do not hear us planning what we intend doing. Then, if it should happen they question you about our whereabouts at certain times and dates, you can seriously claim ignorance of any actions on our part.' He thought a long moment then nodded his head. 'There is something you can do, however.'

He outlined his plan for her part in their attempts to undercut Nathan Wolfgang's plans. Once he finished she agreed and withdrew from the group. Satisfied his endeavours for Ellen's safety and part in the plan to outwit Wolfgang were solid, he turned to the men.

'Now, here is what I have in mind. It may work, it may not. But I think it is worth a try.'

14

Nathan Wolfgang paced his study, smoking a large cigar, and contemplated his past day's move against Ellen Turner and her ranch. He had committed a crime, which in the land where he lived at this day, was against all morals and integrity of the West. He had burned a home, seized a young woman and forced her to leave, and taken her land and her cattle. He knew his actions would cause raised eyebrows, some coldness on the part of other ranchers. But he also knew that, in time, the taste of what he had done would lessen, and only a few would hold it against him beyond two or three years. This was a way of life. It was a hard life in a new, wild and often harsh land. One seized what one wanted! He made his mark known, and the fear of its happening to others would cause many to bury the incident, fearing a comparable situation might bring the same action to their own doorsteps.

He nodded, drawing on the cigar. In time, with him the largest landholder in the territory and with the richest pockets with which to operate, he could see no obstacles impeding his progress toward his goal.

* * *

Homer Ragsdale was angry. To him, it seemed he was angry all the time. He had examined the map, held by the bank, showing the boundaries of the ST ranch, and he found that Mel Lewis was either wrong in his reading of papers in Pierre, regarding the Turner spread, or he was cheating, and lying to the banker.

The ST boundaries, drawn up years ago by the owner, Silas Turner, showed that the mine was indeed on the Turner property. Lewis had assured him it was clear that it was not. This was too much. He yelled to his secretary, a maiden lady of indeterminable age. 'Get word to Mel Lewis, I want to see him. Now!'

* * *

It was a week since Wolfgang had put Ellen Turner on the stage out of Fall Creek. As the stage driver topped a rise in the road, once again he found Hoppy Jackson obstructing the road, holding the reins of a second horse. Standing beside him was Ellen Turner, whom Hoppy and Blue had taken from his stage a few days ago.

'Whoa, drat it.' He drew the stage to a halt. Curious passengers stuck their heads out of the window. Seeing the young woman waiting for the stage, they settled back in their seats.

'Hoppy Jackson, what are you stoppin' me again fer? Don't you know I have a schedule to meet?'

Hoppy spat to one side. 'This here young lady needs a ride into Pierre. We didn't want to ride all the way into town, when she could board the stage here just as well.'

'Waal, since you come all this way out here I guess it's only human kindness to take you on.' The driver smiled beneath a bushy moustache and nodded to Ellen. 'Climb aboard, Miss Turner. I'll get you into Pierre, sooner or later.' He grinned at Hoppy and shook his head. 'I ain't sure what's goin' on, old friend, but I won't tell anyone about this happenin', if you don't.'

Hoppy grinned at him and backed his horse out of the road. Ellen leaned out of the stage's window and waved to him, as the rough-riding vehicle moved on by him. He watched it disappear in its own trail of dust and, leading Ellen's horse, turned onto a thin trail which would lead him back to the ST range.

* * *

Two nights later four shadowy figures moved onto the N slash W headquarters. One slipped up to the big house.

There was a single window showing a light. The other three figures spread out to the barns and sheds. Quietly they searched the buildings and, finding one horse stabled — due to some injury being treated and rested, they turned the animal into a pasture, gave it a slap on the flank and sent it limping off into the darkness.

The three met at the largest barn, the loft of which was full of hay. In one corner, a light flared, a match was touched to a twist of hay, and in a few minutes, flames crept up a wall. The figures left the barn and went to their horses, tethered several yards away. They spread out and began hazing the ranch's remuda, scattering it in the pastures nearby.

The figure on the porch of the main house tried the front door and finding it locked, went to a back door. He eased it open and after a moment of listening, slipped into what was the kitchen. There was the odour of coffee in the air, the smell of freshly baked bread.

Whatever kind of man he might be, Blue mused, he likes his eats.

There was a long hall leading towards the front of the house. Under the crack of a door, about half-way down the hall, was a thin sliver of light. Blue approached the door with silent steps, and, quietly turning the knob, opened it slightly. It was Wolfgang's study. The ranch owner sat in an easy chair, facing away from the door, reading a book from what, to Blue's eyes, was a large library of volumes.

Blue stepped into the room and quietly closed the door behind him. Some slight sound, the change of atmosphere, caused by the opening and closing of the door, brought the rancher around in his chair. His eyes widened and his face blanched.

Blue's sixgun was drawn, the hammer cocked as Wolfgang watched, the dark bore centred upon his forehead.

'Not a sound, Wolfgang,' Blue said softly. 'Just sit still and you won't be hurt.'

'How dare you! How did you get in here? I'll have you in territorial prison for this!'

Blue shook his head. 'You sit still and listen. I am just beginning to repay you for what you did to Ellen Turner. By the time I'm through with you, you'll wish you had never heard of her or the ST spread.'

Blue gestured with his gun. 'Stand up. Put the book down, and turn your back.'

'I won't — '

Swiftly Blue stepped forward and slapped Wolfgang's face with a resounding blow! Blood appeared from his nose. He opened his mouth to yell, but the fist met his lips and smashed them back into his teeth, blood now spurting out of his injured mouth and down over his vest. He groaned. Blue whirled him around and, whipping a bandanna from the man's neck, gagged him with it. Seizing Wolfgang's arms, Blue turned him about and, with a pigging string, tied his hands tightly back of him.

Taking the rancher by the arms, Blue shoved him to a window which overlooked the barns and sheds and the corrals which, at the moment, held no animals. He shoved Wolfgang's face to the glass.

'Now look at the main barn,' he said, his voice tight with disgust and anger. 'Watch your barns, your winter's cattle-feed burn! You think you will get even with me? Through Ellen Turner?' Blue barked a short laugh. 'Who are you going to tell that one man came into your home, tied you up and burned your barns? You've too much pride to tell it right. Oh, I'm not going to kill you this time. But there'll be other times!'

He twisted the now cowering rancher about to face him.

'I'm going now. We'll meet again, and the next time . . . ' The grim cast of Blue's face told Wolfgang that he had made a dangerous enemy. He was lucky he was not a dead man, slouched in his chair, with an unread book in his lap.

Blue marched him over and shoved him down in the chair he had been occupying. He stood before Wolfgang, staring down at the rancher with cold, still, steely eyes.

'Things are going to happen to you, until you will think hell has come to be on your range. I would advise you to make restitution to Ellen Turner for what you have done. If not, then take the consequences like a man, if you are a man!'

With that Blue seized Wolfgang's legs and bound them with another pigging string. He rose and turned to the hallway door, turning back with a cold smile at the rancher.

'You'd better get yourself loose and your crew busy with water-buckets, or you won't have any barns or sheds left.' He closed the door and left the house quickly and silently. He mounted his horse tethered a few yards away, and rode swiftly out toward the pastures where he knew Noah and the other men were scattering N slash W cattle.

By the time the rancher's crew had the fire out, if possible, Ellen Turner's hands would have scattered cattle and horses so it would take hours for them to be rounded up. He smiled grimly at the thought. Before long, Nathan Wolfgang would question whether it was wise to remain in the territory.

15

'Hoppy.' Blue and the elderly cowboy cook, were on guard, sitting on a promontory not far from the shack, 'just how good are you with that cannon of yours?'

Hoppy spat and turned his attention to Blue. 'Wa'al, it's been a long spell since I tested it against wind an' nature. But it's good for five hundred yards in most kind of weather, an' a half-mile, if the wind is right.'

Blue was broodingly silent for long minutes.

'We are in for some trouble, Hoppy, you know that. But I served under a colonel in the war a few years back, who said a good offence was the best defence. I reckon this may be our situation right now. If we're going to keep ahead of Wolfgang, then we're going to have to keep them on edge and off balance. If you are willing, here is what I want you to do.'

Quietly he outlined a plan, Hoppy nodding acceptance from time to time.

* * *

Nathan Wolfgang was furious. He had finally freed himself and found that his crew, with buckets of water, and wet blankets, had beat out the flames on the back side of the barn. Other than scorched boards and some burned hay on the floor of the barn, there was no damage. But, while the entire crew was busy putting out the fire, his remuda was rousted out of the corrals and scattered over the nearby pastures. It took the crew half a day to round up enough horses to gather the rest of the animals into the corrals.

Then a ride out on the range revealed that a selected herd being readied for shipment had been scattered, and would take a week to round up and prepare for the shipment.

He had not yet disclosed to his men, not even Sam Fletcher, his *segundo*, that Blue had entered the main house, tied him up and made him realize how small he was, not only in stature, but in morality, as well. This latter thought, however, brushed him only briefly, then was gone. Morality was measured in the manner by which it benefited him.

He stood on the porch of his large home, smoking one of his ever-present cigars. It was mid-morning. The crew was still gathering and counting the prize herd. He eyed those busy about the corrals and the barn. He moved to the edge of the porch, and there was a loud slap against the boards of the house. Then a 'boom', as though a small cannon had been discharged at a distance. Belatedly he realized someone had fired a rifle at him, and had missed him by a mere foot. He dropped to the porch floor and yelled for his men.

Sam Fletcher came running to the house, seeing his boss stretched out on the boards of the porch. Wolfgang was pale and shaken.

'Someone took a shot at me,' he stammered. 'Nearly killed me. Look, see that bullet-hole in the wall there?' He twisted about and pointed with a shaking finger at the boards where a large projectile had entered, leaving a hole big enough to thrust a finger through.

Fletcher jerked about and looked beyond the barns. The main headquarters of the N slash W ranch lay cupped in a small valley, arranged so to escape the worst of the winters' winds. There were groves of piñon, oak and pine on all sides, rising above the buildings. The valley opened up shallowly onto the closest meadows and then flattened onto the ranges. It was a perfect location for a ranch headquarters, protected from the winds and cold of the winter, with shelter for the grazing animals during the heat of summers. It was also a perfect place for Hoppy Jackson to lay up with his old Sharps .50 rifle and follow through with Blue's suggestion.

'Don't shoot to kill someone,' he had told Hoppy. 'Just harass them, come as close as you can, without hitting someone. We want Wolfgang to know he's in our sights, and we can make him jump or we can drill him, if we want.'

Hoppy had nodded and twisted a grin on his beardy face. 'Got it, boss. Keep 'em jumpy. Leave it up to me.'

'And don't get caught at it,' Blue warned him. 'They will probably be as mad as hornets with their nest poked with a stick.'

'Ya tryin' to teach an ol' dog to suck eggs?' Hoppy lifted an eyebrow at Blue.

'Nope. Just don't want more blood than necessary,' said Blue softly.

A day later Hoppy found his position with a clear field of fire. He had been in place since before dawn. When Wolfgang appeared upon the porch, the old cowboy was shaken with the desire to send his projectile through the body of the rancher, knowing what he had done to Ellen Turner. But he resisted and fired to a point just beyond Wolfgang.

Grinning beneath his handlebar moustache, Hoppy reloaded his old rifle and slipped out of his hiding-place to find another. He knew that the keen eyes of one of the cowpunchers would see the drift of smoke from his weapon, and riders would be sent out to find him.

Two hours later he was a half-mile away from his first hiding-place, lying between two ancient boulders and looking over the main barn lot of the ranch. Nathan Wolfgang was nowhere to be seen, but others were passing back and forth among the sheds, corrals and bunkhouse. One individual came out of the bunkhouse and stood at one corner of the building, shading his eyes and looking intently at the hills around the ranch.

Hoppy's moustache twitched with a grin and he settled down to sighting the Sharps. Centring his sights to a post, just to the right of the observer, he gently caressed the trigger of the old weapon. It roared, and blue smoke drifted about him.

The slug ripped through the post beside the man who was looking for Hoppy and sent splinters into his face. He yelled and dived back into the bunkhouse. Others came running from positions around the ranch house, telling Hoppy that they were on guard, perhaps on pins and needles, waiting for the next shot. He smiled wryly to himself and slipped away to find another vantage point from where to harass the N slash W rancher.

* * *

Mel Lewis and the banker met in the Fall Creek Saloon, and there Ragsdale confronted the marshal concerning the boundary lines of the ST Ranch and the location of the mine.

'You assured me that the mine was on government land,' he growled at Lewis. 'I ran the lines on the map I have in the bank and see that the mine is really on ST land. Just what is your game?' He glared at the former foreman of the ST ranch.

'That map you have is old. Surveys were careless in those days. Why, some old Spanish land-grant maps were as much as a quarter-mile or so off. The surveying is better now, and the map at the land office in Pierre is newer and more up to date.'

Ragsdale eyed him balefully. 'You go out there,' he ordered, 'and bring in some more ore. Go back in the mine and dig some out. I'll take it to Pierre myself and make sure you're not trying to pull a sham on me.'

'Me do that to you? After we decided to be partners in this deal? I'm an honest man, Homer, and you know you can trust me.'

'Get more of the ore, then we'll see.' Ragsdale rose and left the saloon. He was satisfied at this point that his partner in the mining deal was out to skin him. And it took a better man than Mel Lewis to skin Homer Ragsdale — the chief of all 'skinners' himself.

* * *

'Let's go gather up some cattle, boys,' Blue announced, after their meagre breakfast of sourdough biscuits, venison and second-day coffee. Supplies at the shack camp were running low. 'Tonight, I'll slip into town and find us some vittles.'

After eating, filling canteens and saddling their horses, the four, Blue and Noah, with the two men who had joined them, left the camp and rode cautiously onto the N slash W range. Observing a small meadow, formed in a cul-de-sac, Blue realized that Wolfgang was gathering a herd. It would probably be a herd meant for shipment. Wolfgang was running short of money and would need to sell some cattle to fatten his bank account.

Blue rested his forearm on the saddle horn and studied the small herd gathered in the bowl before them.

'I believe that it would be to our advantage,' he told Noah, 'to scatter that herd again. We must try to keep Wolfgang guessing and from meeting his money needs.'

Noah nodded and then pointed with his chin, Indian fashion.

'There's some fellers down there, under them trees kinda outta sight, that might argue with us about rousting their critters. Maybe we had ought to — '

His remark was interrupted by a shout from someone guarding the herd. Almost instantly four men appeared from the trees and were staring up the hill to where the guard was pointing.

'Well, looks like they seen us,' drawled one of the men who had joined with Blue in his struggle against Wolfgang.

Blue grinned wryly. 'Looks like it. Come on, boys, get behind that herd and run it past those rannies. See if we can scatter them right along with their beef.'

He lifted his reins, gigged his horse down over the rim of the cup and pointed it around the slope, to come up back of the herd. The animals were aware something was happening. They stirred restlessly, some bawled and they milled.

Seeing Blue and his crew descending upon the herd and suddenly realizing what they were intending, two of the N slash W hands drew guns and began firing at the racing horses. Their shots went wild, however, and the noise agitated the cattle all the more.

Blue waved for the men to spread out back of the herd; they began whooping and snapping rope-ends at the nervous animals. In what seemed an instant, as so often happened in cattle stampeding, some leaders struck out away from the noise and ropes, and headed for the opening in the cul-de-sac. Suddenly the entire herd stormed after them.

Facing the oncoming cattle, the four Wolfgang riders turned and raced for the nearest copse of trees. Two, seeing some of the rushing animals ploughing and bellowing among the trees, scampered awkwardly in high-heel boots to climb trees or boulders to safety. The other two reached their horses in time and disappeared over the lips of the small cove.

* * *

Once out of the small cup that had contained them, the cattle spread out, slowed down, settled to a walk, and began seeking graze on the flats where they found themselves.

As Blue rode past the copse of trees where two of the Wolfgang riders had sought safety, a body launched itself from behind a boulder and struck him, throwing him from his horse.

Noah and the other men reined in their mounts and turned in time to see Blue struggling with an individual, attempting to throw him to the ground. The two men wrestled and fought while the others crowded about.

'Noah, do we want to break this up?'

asked one of the men. Noah raised a hand, shaking his head.

'Let's see how Blue handles it. If he needs help, we'll put a rope on the rannie.'

Blue had regained his composure. The man was not armed, having lost his weapon in his mad dash through the trees to escape a plunging cow. Angry, he attacked Blue with pin-wheeling punches, which Blue evaded. Watching for an advantage, Blue stepped in under one of the wide swinging blows, and with two quick lefts and rights, knocked the man off his feet. The man leaped up, yelling in anger and met another devastating fist to the jaw, which laid him out, dazed and groping on the ground.

Blue stepped away from him.

'Come on, man, you don't want to fight Wolfgang's battles all by yourself, do you? Go find your horse, and get out of here.' Blue reached his mount which was being held by Noah.

The man rose and staggered and shook his head.

'I reckon I lost my head for a moment,' he muttered and then grinned wryly. 'I was just plumb mad that we let you slip up on us like that.'

'It's over,' Blue said shortly. He mounted and looked down at the Wolfgang rider. 'Go tell your boss that we're gathering up some of Miss Ellen Turner's beef. If he wants to argue about it, take it up with the sheriff of the territory in Pierre.' With that he motioned to Noah and the other men and, gigging his horse, left the man standing dejectedly on the trail.

* * *

Two weeks later the stage driver, coming in from Pierre, pulled his vehicle to a standstill at the place where he had been halted on one of his trips to the capital. He looked at the rider, who sat on his horse in the middle of the road, holding the reins of another horse, saddled and apparently awaiting a rider.

The driver spat over the side and, wiping his mouth, glared at Blue.

'Between you and Hoppy Jackson, I never reach my schedule with this here trap,' he grunted. He turned, leaned over and called down into the stage. 'Miss Ellen, thar's a feller out here holdin' a hoss fer you. Reckon you better get off here. I'll get your valise.'

Ellen Turner stepped from the stage. Her face shining with pleasure, she smiled up at Blue. 'You look good to me, Blue,' she murmured.

He touched his hat and grinned at her. 'And you're a sight for sore eyes, Miss Ellen. I got your horse here for you.'

'Good,' she said, taking her valise from the driver. 'Let's go home.'

16

Blue walked away from the shack which he and the others of the crew had repaired and made half-way usable for an extended stay. Blankets had been strung across one end of the room, giving Ellen Turner a temporary privacy. They all realized this was a brief pause in their attempt to return her to the rightful ownership of her small ranch, now under the control of Nathan Wolfgang. Two men, Bill Kemp and Charlie Shehan, had become accepted as part of the solid group looking for a way of wresting the ST from the clutches of the miserly owner of the N slash W ranch.

He stood looking out over the mesa where their shack perched beneath its blue, far-reaching lift, rising toward the mountains, rough, boulder strewn, but a good place, to hide from Wolfgang's crew who searched for them. Apparently none of the N slash W crew knew about the line shack crouched beneath the craggy lip of the mesa.

He heard the sound of a light footstep and turned to find Ellen approaching him, a blanket draped across her shoulders against the slight chill of the mesa height. She came close and leaned against him and he put an arm about her and drew her close.

They did not speak, but stood, sharing a moment together, before it was time to talk and plan for their next move. He turned her to him and, raising her chin with a gentle finger, lowered his face and kissed her gently. She responded, her lips soft and accepting. Long, slow moments passed before she sighed and settled again in his arms, looking out over the drop of the mesa.

'We found your seed bull,' he told her softly. 'We rounded him up with several other head of your cattle and have them in a small cove hidden just under the mesa about a mile from here. They are all right. I didn't want Wolfgang to round the bull up and sell him.'

She looked at him quietly, love shining in her eyes.

'I trust you to do the right thing, Blue. Now, I have something to tell you. In a week we are going into town, and here's the reason why.' She held his arm and explained her plan. 'Nathan Wolfgang has a big surprise coming for him.'

Blue did not pressure her. She only told him that they could go into town quietly. She would stay with a widow woman in a small house on the outskirts of Fall Creek. He, Hoppy and the rest of the crew would camp out and come into town the day after they arrived there, coming in just in time to meet the stage from Pierre.

The days went slowly. Hoppy returned to the camp.

'I'm outta shells,' he told Blue. 'An' I reckon I put enough holes in that house that if it rains, it'll leak like a sieve.'

Blue nodded. 'That was what I wanted you to do. I'm pretty sure it made Wolfgang think. Now, we're going to do something else.' He explained Ellen's planning, as much as he understood it.

'You slip into town in about three days and make arrangements for Miss Ellen to stay at the Widow Guthrie's house. Things are about to start making Nathan Wolfgang sorry he ever touched an inch of the ST range.'

* * *

Mel Lewis had no intention of going back into the mine on the further edge of the ST range. The assay had proven only a smattering of gold and that not of sufficiently good quality to make it worth the mining. He had other thoughts and after a few days away from town, causing Ragsdale to reason he was following orders about collecting new ore, he slipped back, in the darkest part of the night.

It did not take him long to break the lock on the back door of the bank, and he knew where Ragsdale kept a small notepad that contained the combination to the elderly safe. Within a few minutes, working under the flickering flame of a small candle, he had the safe open. With quivering fingers he lifted out bundles of bills, and stuffed them into a burlap bag brought for that purpose.

He decided against taking the heavy bag of coins on account of its weight. He was ready to leave Fall Creek, and he wanted nothing to slow his departure. A saddled horse awaited back of the bank, along with another packed with necessary items with which he could camp for several days, before catching a stage out of the territory.

He closed the door behind him quietly, mounted his horse and, taking the lead rope of the pack horse, disappeared in the shadows of the trees along the trail leading out of town.

He was certain no one was up and

about the streets of the town to see him leave. But he was wrong.

Hoppy Jackson stood in the shadows of the livery, where he was bunking, after making arrangements for Ellen Turner's visit with the Widow Guthrie. He recognized Lewis as the marshal moved out of the shadows of the bank building and onto the trail leading out of Fall Creek. He logged this into his mind along with other information he had gathered to alert Blue.

* * *

The day after Ellen Turner came into Fall Creek and made her way to the widow's home, the stage arrived from Pierre. It held three passengers; a travelling salesman, with his valise of catalogues and samples, a rancher's wife, returning from a trip East, and a tall, elderly, gaunt man, wearing an ancient duster over dark clothes.

Judge James Monroe Wesley had arrived from the state capital on what was assumed to be his routine visit to conduct hearings awaiting his attention.

That was the secondary reason for his visit. The first reason was in response to a lengthy discussion with Ellen Turner when she was in Pierre. Judge Wesley and Silas Turner had been friends for years. The elderly lawman was deeply interested in what was occurring in Fall Creek and its territory, detrimental to the welfare of the daughter of his old friend.

The judge placed his valise in the room reserved for him over the mercantile. Washing up at the basin made ready for him under a mirror against one end of the room, the elderly lawman sighed and straightened. He was tired from the journey out of Pierre. He grimaced and mused, the old bones take a beating on that rough vehicle. Replacing his hat he left the room, closing the door firmly behind him.

Homer Ragsdale looked up as his secretary, a widow of indeterminable years, knocked and entered.

'Judge Wesley is here to see you,' she told him, nervously. 'He's outside right now.'

'The judge? He isn't due here for a month, at least. What's he coming in so early for?'

The secretary shrugged. 'I don't know, Mr Ragsdale.' She stepped aside and held the door wider. 'Here he is.'

Judge Wesley strode into the room, nodding courteously to the secretary and then pausing before Ragsdale's desk.

'Good morning, Judge.' The banker rose from his seat and came around the desk, his hand outstretched. 'It is always nice to have you in town. Here,' he pushed a ladder-back chair around and gestured to it, 'have a seat.'

The judge shook his head. 'Haven't got the time to palaver long, Homer,' the lawman said. 'I want you to send a rider out to Nathan Wolfgang's ranch and tell him I want him and his foreman here, for a hearing, about noon tomorrow. No later, or I'll have them arrested for ignoring the call of the circuit judge.'

Ragsdale eyed the judge warily. 'Certainly, Judge. I'll see to it immediately.' He lifted an eyebrow questioningly, 'This is urgent business, eh? Anything you can discuss?'

Judge Wesley mistrusted the banker. He knew of deals made by the banker which skirted the edges of propriety as well as legality.

'Only to tell you, Homer, that I want you to be present tomorrow and have available for the hearing any papers dealing with Silas Turner's purchase of the ranch. Also, any papers his daughter, Ellen Turner, might have signed since his death.'

Suddenly there were beads of sweat on Ragsdale's forehead. He wiped them away with a bandanna and then shrugged. 'No problem, Judge. I'll be there. Now, just which papers is it that you want?'

When the judge was gone, Ragsdale

sat back heavily in his chair and shuddered. He did not like what he had been ordered to do, but neither did he enjoy the vision of his being in territorial prison for whatever reason. He called his secretary and instructed her to bring the papers on the ST ranch, as well as any other paper signed by the father or Ellen. While she was doing so he hurried to the saloon and within a few minutes had a roustabout on a livery horse on his way to the N slash W ranch.

* * *

A knock on the back door of Widow Guthrie's home brought Blue to his feet. He nodded to the widow to answer the knock. The elderly woman opened the door and then nodded to Blue where he sat at the kitchen table with Ellen.

'It's the judge,' she said to Ellen. She opened the door wider. 'Come on in, Judge. It's good to see you again.'

He smiled and shook her hand. 'It's been a long time, Sarah,' he said. 'I came because I needed a slice of that deep-dish apple-pie you make.'

She blushed and almost curtsied. 'Believe it or not, Judge, I have one ready to slice. Before you leave you'll have all the pie you can eat.'

The judge came into the room and Ellen rose from the table to meet him. He hugged her and then backed away, holding her hands. 'I took a day to study the situation from the capital. This Wolfgang fellow has been in shady deals before. He is known to have run out, beaten or even killed smaller ranchers and farmers where he desired their land. I think this is what he has in mind here in Fall Creek territory. We'll have a talk with him tomorrow.' He turned to Blue.

'I do not believe we have met. I understand that Miss Ellen here, and one old scoundrel I know, Hoppy Jackson, broke you out of jail recently. Well, we'll take the problems here one at a time. We'll discuss your being in the jail later.'

He held out his hand and Blue, grasping it, was satisfied that here was a man. His grip was firm and strong, and he looked Blue in the eye as they shook. 'Miss Ellen seems to put a lot of trust and belief in you. I hope you are deserving of that faith.'

Blue nodded, as they released their grips. 'Judge, I will do all in my powers, such as they are, to help Miss Ellen. Mrs Guthrie has just made a fresh pot of coffee. Won't you have a seat, and a cup of the coffee? Miss Ellen has told us part of what you talked about in Pierre.'

Seated, with a large mug of coffee in his hands, the judge proceeded to outline what procedures he would use in the hearing the following day. When he was finished, Blue questioned him closely for several minutes. Finally, satisfied that the judge was on the right track, he relaxed and, over a second cup of coffee, listened to several tales of the old judge's experiences in this wild and, as yet, untamed territory.

★ ★ ★

His secretary, standing before his desk, wringing her hands, watched the banker pale and then grow rosy with anger. His jowls shook with his anxiety.

'What do you mean, that the safe has been robbed?'

'Mr Ragsdale, you sent me to get some papers having to do with the ST ranch. I . . . I found them, all right, but sir, if you had any money in the safe, it's all gone.'

'I had five thousand dollars in bills in the safe and a bag of coins among which were several five, ten and twenty dollar gold pieces.'

'The bag of coins is still there,' she murmured, her eyes filling with tears. 'And all the papers you wanted are there.' She laid them on the corner of his desk. 'But, there's no bills of any kind.'

Heaving from his chair, Ragsdale lumbered into the small room back of his office. Kneeling before the safe, he searched it carefully. The books and papers were disturbed somewhat, and the bag of coins was there. But, as the secretary had said there were no bills. He knew there had been bundles of several denominations, counted into five-hundred-dollar groups, and tied with string. Only about five-hundred dollars had been loose, to use as needed during daily business. He closed the safe door and returned to his desk. Shaken by the discovery of the theft, he began examining the papers that he held concerning the ST ranch and its former owner, Silas Turner. So far as he could ascertain everything was in order. On top of the papers was a signed agreement by Ellen Turner, to sell the ST to Nathan Wolfgang for a stated sum of money. Ragsdale examined the papers with half his mind. The other half was speculating as to whom it might have been that robbed his safe.

He called his secretary into the office.

'Send someone to Mel Lewis and have him here within the hour. He might be able to throw some light on who robbed me — robbed the safe.'

* * *

Mel Lewis was ten miles from Fall Creek. He had traveled carefully the entire night, and now was hidden in a copse of pine and piñon trees, preparing a scant meal from supplies he had brought with him. The saddle-bags, containing the bank's money, lay on his blankets by the small fire he had built to boil coffee. He looked at them with a satisfactory expression on his face. He could cut a big swath in Chicago or San Francisco with that money. Put himself up in a small business, travel in Europe, do whatever he wished to do. For the first time in his life, he felt free, no longer bound by job, morals or need of money. It was all there, in those saddle-bags!

He unrolled his blankets, poured himself a cup of coffee and sat gloating on his fortune.

As he was gloating, Hoppy Jackson was talking with Higgens, the Fall Creek Saloon owner. A roustabout came ambling into the saloon and up to the bar.

'Anyone seen Mel Lewis around? Homer Ragsdale wants to see him right away. Might be some marshalin' job he wants done.'

Hoppy looked at him. 'What d'ya reckon Ragsdale wants with him? There something happened here needin' Lewis's attention?'

The roustabout shrugged. 'He gave me a dollar to find him, but no one seems to have seen him since last night here in the saloon.'

Hoppy shrugged. He had not seen Lewis, not in the daylight. But he was now certain that the figure he had seen leaving town about one o'clock in the morning was the marshal.

* * *

Blue awakened from a deep sleep near midnight. He was rolled in his blankets, under a large pine, back of the Guthrie home. Hoppy, Noah and the others had bunked down in one room above the mercantile.

He awakened from a dream in which he surveyed again a strange hoofprint and knew, without doubt, that the print held the key to the murder of Silas Turner.

17

Judge Wesley held the hearing in the saloon. At nine o'clock he entered the establishment and, having informed Higgens of his need of the space, approached the bar. He picked up an empty beer-mug and rapped it three times on the wood.

'This bar's closed until further notice,' he declared. There were already a dozen men in the saloon, anticipating the hearing, and enjoying an early morning beer.

Higgens came around from behind the bar and pushed a table before it, with a chair back to the bar, and one beside it. The judge thanked him and proceeded to seat himself back of the table. He laid out a pad of paper, some pencils, and a beaten old copy of Blackstone's 'Commentaries'. As he did so, the bar's front door opened and

Nathan Wolfgang, along with his foreman, Sam Fletcher, strode into the room. Nathan marched up to the table and stared down at the judge.

'What's this all about, Wesley?' he growled, glaring down at the old lawman. 'Dragging me and my foreman in here for some penny-ante something or other.'

Judge Wesley eyed him coolly. 'I am Judge Wesley to you, when I'm holding a meeting such as this and am in charge. You will address me as such. As to why I desired the presence of you and your foreman, that will be related at the proper time. Now, be seated and be quiet unless I call upon you.' The lawman's eyes met those of the rancher without flinching.

Wolfgang stiffened and then with a final glare at the judge, turned away and went to an unoccupied table, where he seated himself. His foreman followed and sat across from him.

The judge tapped his table with his pencil. 'This hearing is now in session. I have come here to listen to a serious complaint of one of your citizens.' He looked about. 'I note that the marshal, Mel Lewis, is absent. Was he not alerted to the meeting?'

Hoppy Jackson rose from half-way back in the room. 'No sir, Judge. He ain't in town, apparently. No one seemed to have seen him.'

The judge nodded. 'Very well. Then, in the absence of the marshal, Hoppy Jackson, I hereby appoint you as marshal for this meeting. You will see that it is carried on with decorum. There will be no loud talking, cussing, or using the spittoons. Either get rid of your cuds, now, or swallow your juice.'

There were growls, and then several of the men rose and sought spittoons and emptied their mouths of tobacco. When the room had settled down, the judge tapped again for quiet.

'I have before me the complaint of a landowner in the territory near Fall Creek environs that one Nathan Wolfgang has invaded her property, burned her buildings and rustled her cattle. The ST ranch hereby asked for relief by law from such actions. Is there anyone here who will rise to this complaint?'

Nathan Wolfgang was on his feet. 'That is an outright and scandalous lie, your honor. The ST ranch and all its holdings were sold to me by the present owner, a Miss Ellen Turner, complete and outright. I have a signed agreement to the action. I resent greatly such calumny of my good name and demand an apology immediately.' Wolfgang stretched to the limit of his meagre height and stood awaiting the judge's rebuttal.

Judge Wesley eyed him thoughtfully. 'Are you saying you did none of the things you are accused of?'

'Absolutely, your honor. I am an honest, hard-working man and all I have has come by my own efforts throughout my lifetime.'

The judge picked up a paper from the desk. He read it slowly and then looked over to where Homer Ragsdale sat, near the center of the room.

'I have here a document, signed by Miss Turner, owner of the ST ranch, whereby she sells all her property, holdings and cattle to you for a ridiculous price. The local banker, Mr Ragsdale, has brought the paper forward at my request. Will you identify the document?'

Wolfgang hesitated and darted a glance over at Ragsdale and then took the paper from the judge's hand. He pretended to read it carefully and then handed it back to the old lawman. 'That is the article signed by Miss Turner. Her signature is appended on the bottom line.'

The judge nodded slowly and then spoke. 'You have stated that you are an honest and upright man. Then you swear before this company and to the representative of the law of this territory, that this is a true and acceptable signature of the then owner of the ST ranch?'

Wolfgang hesitated and then nodded,

staring the judge directly in the face. 'Yes, sir, I do.'

The judge looked at him for a long moment and then nodded slowly. 'Very well. Then you will not mind if I call someone besides yourself to attest to the legality of this document?' He turned and nodded to the saloon owner, Higgens, who was leaning against the wall adjacent to the door of a back room of the establishment. Higgens pushed away from the wall and went to the door.

Wolfgang turned and shot a hot glance at Homer Ragsdale whose face was suddenly pale and sweaty. The banker looked down at the hat in his hand and did not meet the gaze of the rancher.

Higgens opened the door and Ellen Turner and Blue stepped into the room. Blue moved over to one side where he could see both Wolfgang and his foreman, Fletcher. He put his eyes to Fletcher's face, and the foreman sneered at him boldly.

Wolfgang was shaken. He staggered back from the judge's table and then caught himself and straightened. His eyes never left the face of the young woman as she came forward to meet the judge.

The judge held out the paper which he had discussed with both Ragsdale and Wolfgang.

'Miss Turner, I have discussed the problem you outlined for me recently, concerning the local banker, who held the paper, and Mr Wolfgang, who swears that you sold him your property, free and clear. That the stated amount of money on this paper is now held in the local bank for your use. My question to you is this: is this your signature?'

Ellen took the paper from him and glanced down at the signature on the bottom line. 'This is not my signature, your honor.' She picked a pencil from the table and, beneath her name on the paper, wrote her name swiftly. She handed the paper to the judge.

'My signature and the one on the paper do not match in any way. The paper was forged with my name.'

Ragsdale was on his feet. 'Now, see here, young woman. I saw you sign the paper — '

'Judge!' A woman rose from the back of the saloon and came forward hesitantly. Her hands were clasped nervously before her. Ragsdale turned and saw her approaching, and his face blanched.

'Just who are you, and what do you know about this?' Judge Wesley asked her, gesturing for her to come closer. 'Why do you come forward?'

The woman stood before him, pale and shaking, her hands twisting in a handkerchief. 'Judge, your honor, that ain't her signature. I know for sure it ain't.'

'Who is this woman!' yelled Wolfgang. 'Why is she allowed — '

The judge pointed a finger into Wolfgang's face. 'You shut up and sit down, or I will hold you in contempt of this court. If that happens you will pay the court a stiff fine and perhaps spend a few days in jail to allow you to consider your sins!'

Nathan Wolfgang was unused to being talked to in this manner. He was always in charge of whatever he was involved in, and this judge was questioning his integrity and ordering him around like a mere flunkey. He sputtered and his eyes bulged with fury. He started to speak and the judge interfered.

'Hoppy Jackson, as marshal *pro tem* of this court, if that man makes one more outburst, you will seize him and take him to that so-called jail this town affords!'

'Yes, sir, Judge, your honor! I'll do it, if he even looks like he wants to rattle off some more.' Hoppy moved from his stance midway the saloon and came to stand near the rancher.

'Now,' the judge spoke gently to the woman. 'What is it you wish to tell this court?'

She glanced hurriedly at the banker, whose eyes were on the floor. 'Miss Turner didn't sign that paper, Judge. The banker, Mr Ragsdale there, he told me to do it. Said if I didn't I'd not have any job left. Judge, I'm a widow with two kids. That job meant all the income I had. But I couldn't stand by and see Miss Turner hurt from something I did, even if I was fired for speakin' up.'

The judge nodded. 'Thank you. What is your name, my dear? Just for the court record.'

'Maude Flynn, your honor. I've been a widow since the War. My husband was killed at Antietam in '62. I need the money, but I ain't no cheat nor no liar. He made me do it!'

The judge nodded. 'Thank you, Mrs Flynn. You are a brave woman and I will see to it that you will have employment before I leave Fall Creek.' She nodded, and returned to her seat, weeping silently into her handkerchief.

The judge turned his attention to the banker. 'Mr Ragsdale, I hereby order you to remain after this hearing is over. I have something more to say to you!

'Now, Mr Wolfgang.' The judge turned his attention back to the rancher. 'According to what Miss Turner tells me, you invaded her property, burned her buildings, kidnapped her and put her on a stage against her will and confiscated her cattle and holdings, land which was filed on and proven up according to the directions of the United States Homesteading programme.' He eyed the rancher grimly. 'What do you say for yourself before I give my rendering for the court?'

Nathan Wolfgang rose from his seat, shaking with anger. He threw back his head and glared at the old lawman.

'I bought the ranch and holdings from Miss Turner. The money for the purchase is in the local bank. She held land upon which the railroad would extend its spur for this part of the territory, and thereby would keep all the other ranchers away, charging them to cross her land for cattle shipment. With me — '

The judge interrupted him. 'Mr Wolfgang, you have not kept up with the activities of the territorial capital. The railroad will not come through the Fall Creek area. They found a better roadbed on the other side of the mountains. The railroad spur you had arranged for yourself will miss this area by forty miles.'

For the first time the diminutive rancher was taken aback. His mouth sagged open and his eyes bulged. He gasped for breath and, reaching for his chair, sat down heavily.

The judge eyed him grimly and continued. 'Mr Wolfgang, I hereby find you guilty of the claims against you. You have stolen, bullied, kidnapped and lied. And all for naught. I hereby order you to do the following: bring all ST cattle back to the Turner ranch. Miss Turner will tell the court how much it will cost to replace her destroyed holdings, and you will place that amount in the local bank for her use, as she sees need. You will apologize to her in public and pay a subsequent fine for falsifying documents, even to the point of forging a bill of sale for your own benefit. Furthermore — '

Sam Fletcher leaped to his feet. 'On your feet, boys!' he yelled. At his voice three N slash W hands leaped up and each of them drew a handgun. Fletcher drew his own.

'Come on, boss,' he grated to Wolfgang. 'There's no 'furthermores' nor anything else.' He waggled the nose of his gun at the crowd. 'We are leavin' an',' he sneered at Ellen Turner, 'you'll be hearin' from us again — soon!'

18

When Fletcher drew his sixgun Blue stepped aside from Ellen and started to draw. She caught his arm.

'No, Blue! There's too many. They'll kill all of us. Let this time pass.'

She felt the strength of his arm under her hand, the tight quivering of his muscles straining against his judgement to wait it out. His face was taut with a deep, controlled anger. But he listened to her, realizing that if a shoot-out started, Ellen would be one of the targets Fletcher and his companions would seek out. But he did not relax. His green eyes glinted with suppressed anger and his gaze took in all of the N slash W men who were involved. Grimly he thought: there will be another day!

Nathan Wolfgang led his crew out of the saloon, Fletcher going last, his sixgun covering the room.

'Every one just stay put,' he snarled, 'an' maybe you won't get plugged. Come out this door in the next ten minutes and you will get shot!'

As the last of the N slash W men left the saloon, the batwing doors swinging shut behind them, Higgens caught Blue's eye and nodded to him.

'You people get out the back. I know your horses are there, so get out of town, now. The judge will be all right here until the Wolfgang crew leaves. But you all ought to be on your way.'

Blue nodded. Taking Ellen's arm he moved her to the door. Hoppy had come to the front and stood near the judge during the last few minutes. His face was flushed with anger and frustration, but he had held himself in check.

'Thanks, Judge,' Blue said. 'I'm sorry you were put into such a position. Those are dangerous men.'

The judge nodded and gestured. 'Get going and make yourselves safe. I will do what I can from my position. I'm thinking that it would not be amiss to have a federal marshal visit here and make contact with Wolfgang. That man must be stopped!'

Blue, with Ellen beside him and Hoppy following, eased out of the back door. Noah was mounted and holding the reins of three horses. In a moment the four of them, led by Blue, followed back alleys of the town, coming out on the trail leading from the town to where they would disappear into the coulees and canyons leading to the line shack beneath the lip of the mesa.

They were seen leaving. Fletcher, anticipating their action, left one of his crew to watch and to follow. The man saw Blue and his party leave town, striking out upon the trail toward the mesa.

* * *

As Blue led Ellen and Hoppy through the trails that led to their hide-away shack, the man Fletcher had deputed to follow them, did so, staying well back, keeping his eye on the hoofprints of their passing. When finally they reached the line shack, he eyed the area intently and then faded back into the landscape, hurrying to report to Wolfgang the location of the ST owner and crew.

* * *

Back at their shack, with the horses cared for, and Hoppy grumping about the stove preparing an evening meal, Ellen and Blue wandered out to the lip of the mesa and stood looking out over the darkening scene.

'That secretary, Mrs Flynn, came up to me just before we left,' said Ellen. 'She told me that she had heard the banker Ragsdale and Mel Lewis talking. They had a scheme to take over an old mine just inside my property, not far from here. They thought there was gold in it.'

Blue looked at her. 'Is there gold there?'

She shook her head. 'No. There never was. Whoever worked it first found only 'fools' gold'. My father said it was called pyrites. No good for anything he could think of.'

'Then Lewis shammed the banker. I'll bet he knew the mine was no good, and was going to take the banker for a roll of money. Then he found out there was no gold, and left town with whatever the banker paid him.'

Hoppy came the door of the shack and called to them. 'Spuds are on. Come an' get it.'

* * *

Judge Wesley knocked on the bank door early on the morning following the hearing. Maude Flynn opened the door and stepped back to let him enter.

He removed his hat and nodded to her. 'Mrs Flynn. It is a pleasure to see you this morning. I wonder if you would tell Mr Ragsdale that I am here to see him.'

He noted her eyes were red, teary from recent weeping.

'He isn't here, your honor. I came in and he was not here.' She led him to the wide-open office door. He stepped in and saw the disarray of a hurried packing. The safe door was open and only a few unimportant papers, bills, ledger pages and an old magazine from Chicago lay about the floor.

He sighed. 'He has absconded with the bank's papers, and whatever money he had, which belonged not to him, but to those trusting him with their savings.'

The secretary shook her head. 'Just papers and such, your honor. The bank was robbed the night before the hearing. He told me not to say anything about it.'

'Well, just leave it as it is. Mrs Flynn. Lock the doors when you leave. And by the way, I will be leaving at noon tomorrow. In the meanwhile I will see about some employment for you.'

She put her hands to her face, beginning to weep again.

'Thank you, Judge, I will be so grateful.'

With a pat on her shoulder the elderly judge left the building. He shook his head. No one would probably ever know who took the money, unless the robber was caught and confessed to the crime. That Mel Lewis, the strangely absent marshal, was mixed up in some deal with the banker seemed reasonable to assume. Both had disappeared, one with money apparently, and one with important papers. The Fall Creek bank was locked up and money belonging to ranchers in the territory, along with mortgages, loan instruments and other papers, was gone.

He shook his head. Sometimes the action of individuals appointed to safeguard the needs of a community betrayed those who placed trust in them. When this happened the community was destroyed and many innocents given insurmountable problems to solve. Fall Creek had placed its trust in a banker and a lawman, and each had broken faith with those who had looked upon them as leaders.

* * *

Blue sat on the doorstep of the shack, surveying the area around it.

The lip of the mesa hung darkly above and behind the shack. A copse of piñon and pine formed a clump about a hundred yards to one side. In front of the shack was a flat area, strewn with large boulders and with ditches formed by the run-off of rain from the mesa.

If I knew I was going to be required to guard this place, where would I stand? Where would I place men with rifles or handguns to protect the shack from invaders? He looked about him, brooding. The shack itself would be little or no protection, with its weather-eroded boards and tinder-dry roof. Yet, the element of surprise lay with those protecting themselves from a concerted charge.

He stirred and went inside. He motioned to Hoppy.

'Get Kemp and Shehan over here. There's some planning needs to be done.'

19

It was late afternoon. The heat from the sun was gone, the light across the mesa was lessening. The only sounds were the snuffling of horses in the corral back of the shack. A crow, disturbed and apparently on guard for his flock, gave a raucous squawk and lifted from the branches of a tall pine.

There came the muted sounds of quietly moving horses and the squeak of leather of someone dismounting, then the tinkle of some metal jarring against a brushing object.

Suddenly there was a yell! Nathan Wolfgang emerged from a clump of bushes to one side of the shack and yelled:

'Get them, boys! Blast that shack off the mesa! Shoot to kill!'

Nathan Wolfgang was crazed with frustration and anger. He had been humiliated before the very people he had ruthlessly treated or ignored. That judge had the nerve to think he could order him to give back the ST cattle, and reimburse that slut, Ellen Turner, so she might rebuild her holdings. And, to cap it all, the railroad was not building a line through this part of the range. All he had planned for the future was thwarted. And to his anger-twisted mind, the only thing he could think of doing was to rid the territory of the cause of his dilemma: get rid of Ellen Turner, take over the ST and its cattle, and let Pierre send all the federal marshals they wished — he was in control; as the old books had told concerning kingdoms years ago, he was the king of all he surveyed! And if he were not so presently, he would eventually make it so!

He grimly told Sam Fletcher: 'Get the boys together, we're going to take care of Turner and her crew and get it over with!'

Fletcher demurred slightly. 'Right,

boss. But be careful around that Blue fellow. He's slick with a pistol.'

Wolfgang snorted. 'Just a run-down-at-the heels, second-hand cowpoke. He'll be no trouble.'

Now he stood and directed a fusillade of bullets into the line shack. When the smoke cleared, he watched intently. There was no movement, no returning fire from the shack.

'Come on, boys,' he yelled, leaping into the clear. 'They're hiding in there. We'll smoke them out.'

Pushed by a cursing Sam Fletcher, five men rose from the bushes and trees before the shack, and gathered about Wolfgang.

'Come on, boys! Let's get them!'

He shook his fist at the shack and stepped out, the men somewhat reluctantly following. They spread out and approached the shack their rifles ready. Some glanced about themselves warily. But all moved forward. Wolfgang stopped them.

'Here. Pour it into that shack until it

falls about their ears!'

The N slash W crew did as ordered. Some knelt, others stood, straddle-legged, and emptied their rifles into the shack. The ramshackle door fell, its leather hinges shredded by the bullets.

As the firing lessened, Blue stepped from behind a large pine fifty feet to one side of them.

'Now, it's our turn! Give them some of what they intended for us,' he yelled. He knelt and sighting upon one of the N slash W crew who was turning his rifle in his direction, he fired. The rifle cracked and before the man could turn, Blue's bullet smashed through his chest and heart. He screamed, dropped his rifle and fell writhing on the ground.

Blue had placed everyone strategically. From a boulder opposite Blue, Hoppy rose and his ancient Sharps .50 bellowed. Another of Wolfgang's crew fell, his head partly torn off by the impact of the huge bullet. Coolly the old man began to load his cannon again, his eyes narrowed to find his next victim,

Kemp, Shehan, and Noah began firing from separate positions. The Wolfgang crew was surrounded. Even Ellen Turner, holding a carbine, watched from behind a large rock. She levelled her rifle but did not fire. The barrage of the ST men had downed three N slash W men. Two threw down their pieces and held up their hands, surrendering.

'Come on, boss!' Sam Fletcher yelled. He seized Wolfgang by an arm and they ran, dodging bullets, until they were hidden by the copse of trees in front of the shack.

Silence descended on the mesa. Blue rose and approached the two surrendered men, his rifle held easily upon them.

'You boys through your fracas now?' he asked, his voice soft and deadly.

One of them nodded. 'We're done, boss. We was just doin' what we was ordered to do.'

Blue nodded, his face grim. 'So they always say. You can always walk away and wash your hands of a shady, mean deal like this one.' He walked over and drew their guns from their holsters and threw them into the brush several feet away. 'Now, you two just hunker down there and be quiet until I decide what to do with you.' Neither of them argued; they moved over to a boulder and squatting, leaned against it.

Blue examined the two bodies on the ground. Both were dead.

'Life lost because a greedy old man pushed them into something he wanted done.' His tone was disgusted. He stood and looked down at the two squatting men.

'You'll get your horses and tie these two on theirs. Take them to Wolfgang and let him bury them. And tell Wolfgang that the next time we meet, he will be the target, not his men.'

Kemp went with the two men and brought up the horses. The bodies were tied onto their respective horses.

Blue nodded to them. 'Now get out of the territory. If I ever see you again you are dead men!'

The two did not answer, but hurriedly mounted and, leading the animals holding their lifeless burdens, they disappeared into the forest, heading back to the N slash W range.

'We have hid out long enough,' Blue told his crew. 'We're going into town and work this thing out with Wolfgang. There isn't a marshal but we can make citizen arrests until the town council appoints one. Undoubtedly Lewis robbed the bank and took off. I suspect Ragsdale has made himself scarce also.' He looked at Ellen. 'I'm sorry I have put you into harm's way, Miss Ellen. But I think now that we have to come out in the open and get this done with. The judge may send a federal marshal down from Pierre. If so, then he can take over.'

She came over to him and touched his arm, her eyes shining with her feelings for him. Hoppy saw the look and his moustache twitched in a sly grin.

'I'll go to Mrs Guthrie's, I will be safe there. And I give you freedom to act as you see fit for the ST ranch. I trust you.' She looked around the group. 'I trust all of you.'

Kemp and Shehan squirmed in embarrassment and nodded.

'We're for you, Miss Ellen.'

* * *

Blue was awakened the next morning by a yell from the edge of the clearing before the shack. With sixgun in hand he eased the door open, crouched low and peered around the edge.

'Hello the shack,' the voice yelled again. A man stood at the edge of the clearing holding a white cloth on a stick. Blue opened the door and stepped out, his sixgun held low against his leg. He would not put it past Wolfgang to use a flag of truce and to creep in under it with a surprise attack.

'What do you want?' Blue asked, his eyes searching the area about the man, looking for concealed gunmen.

'Fletcher said to tell you that he'll meet you in front of the Fall Creek Saloon, at sundown, day after tomorrow. It'll be just you an' him.'

20

Blue walked to the stall where his horse was being kept while in Fall Creek. He entered the stall and spent some time grooming the animal and seeing that there was plentiful feed. As he stepped out of the stall he noticed a fine-looking animal in a stall across from him. He approached to get a better look at the animal, when a hoofprint caught his attention. He knelt and ran his fingers over the print, noticing what seemed to be a flaw or a small crack in the shoe. And the print indicated an off-centred stride of the animal. He rose and looked at the horse contemplatively.

At the front of the livery the attendant was grooming a small buggy-mare. As Blue approached him he ceased his brushing and looked at Blue.

'That's a fine-looking horse back there about three stables on the left-hand side. Who owns it?'

'Oh, him? Beautiful animal, ain't he.' The livery attendant told Blue the name of the owner. Blue nodded his thanks and left, going back to the Widow Guthrie's house for breakfast.

Blue had just finished his second cup of coffee. He pushed back his chair and reached for his sack of Bull Durham tobacco. He hesitated and looked across at Mrs Guthrie, dropping his hand.

'Oh, go on and smoke,' the widow told him. 'My old man smoked a smelly old pipe. Cigarettes aren't nearly as bad.'

Ellen, sitting beside him, laughed. 'Most would have gone on without asking,' she said. 'It's second nature — a cup of java and a quirly to follow.'

He grinned, took out the tobacco and reached for his corn-shuck papers.

There was a knock on the door of the kitchen. Mrs Guthrie looked at them quizzically.

'Who could that be this early?' she murmured, going to the door. She opened it and stepped aside, startled to see Higgens, the saloon keeper, standing there. He tipped his hat to her.

'Mrs Guthrie, pardon my comin' so early, but I need to talk to Blue, if he is here.'

'Come on in. Would you like a cup of coffee?'

He shook his head. 'No ma'am, thankee just the same.' He looked at Blue. 'I just heard, from a drunk N slash W cowpoke, that when you meet Fletcher today, you're goin' to be whipsawed. There'll be some others hidin' nearby an' you won't have a chance.'

Ellen gasped, her hand going to her mouth.

'Oh, Blue, can't you call it off? They'll shoot you to pieces.' Tears hung on her lashes. He reached over, took her hand and held it gently.

'Thank you, Higgens. I think we can figure out something to make things more even. Don't you get yourself in trouble over this.'

Higgens shook his head. 'Doin' only what's right, Blue. I hate to see good men cheated on and especially when this is so important.'

Blue finished his coffee and rose from the table. 'Thank you, Higgens. I get the picture and we'll be ready.'

* * *

The sun was slowly disappearing behind the ridges of the Black Hills which cupped Fall Creek in a full circle. The slopes were reddened and then dull pink, giving away to deep blue and purple. Out on the foothills coyotes began their yelping and quarreling over territorial rights.

Blue stepped from the porch of the Guthrie home and strolled to the main street of Fall Creek. Word of the coming gunfight had spread and there were small clusters of townsfolk standing before the saloon, the mercantile, and leaning against buildings along the street.

He finished the quirly and crushed the smouldering ash beneath a boot-heel. Straightening, he shifted his sixgun into a better reach and slid it in and out of the leather a few times to make certain there would be no drag at the last, crucial, moment.

Sam Fletcher emerged from the saloon, wiping foam of his final beer from his mouth. He laughed at some quip by an acquaintance standing nearby and looked up to see Blue approaching down the street toward him. A grimace of sudden fear crossed Fletcher's face.

'That's about close enough, Blue,' Fletcher's strong voice broke out. The crowd followed him down the street, some slowly dropping out as the dire moment approached.

Blue paused. 'Fletcher, I know who killed the ST boss so his own boss would have a free hand in taking her ranch. It was you, Fletcher, and you are to pay the price. Die here, or go to jail.'

'Now, who is there to take me to jail?

We ain't got no law in Fall Creek. An' the sheriff ain't sendin' no deputies this far.' Fletcher leaned back and laughed in Blue's face.

Moving his hand slightly, Blue opened a jacket-pocket and brought from it a small, circular gold star. Slowly he pinned it on his jacket.

'There is law here now, Fletcher. I am an appointed Deputy United States Federal Marshal. I am arresting you for the murder of Silas Turner, owner of the ST ranch. Put down your weapons and we will go into this further in the confines of the jail.'

'Like hell we will!' screamed Fletcher. 'Get 'im boys. No little gold star is going to stand in my way!' And as he spoke his hand flashed down to his gun-butt.

He yelled in raging fury and, leveling the guns at Blue, began triggering them as fast as possible.

Nathan Wolfgang appeared at the corner of Higgens's saloon. He leveled a beautiful piece costing thousands of dollars in European shooting circles. But as he leveled the weapon, Noah stepped from the opposite corner and the ancient fifty-calibre drilled the rancher plumb centre, blowing away his insides and splattering a group of onlookers who received copious fall-out from the cannon's ferocity.

Another N slash W ranny appeared on the roof of the mercantile to fire down upon the ST men. At a corner of the saloon was Bill Kemp, and as the man on the roof trained his rifle on Blue, Kemp fired. The man rose up and then, dropping his rifle, fell downward onto Main Street, dying as he fell.

Fletcher was firing quickly, too quickly, missing Blue, scattering dirt and gravel on his boots.

Blue turned sideways, raising his sixgun smoothly. As Fletcher fired his fourth round, Blue fired. Fletcher yelled and staggered backwards, falling to the street. Blood gushed from above his belt, the bullet drilling him through front to back.

His last shot struck Blue in the left side. Blue staggered, fell and rolled over, groaning with pain. As he rolled, Fletcher lifted his pistol to fire again. Dazed and in agonizing pain, Blue gritted his teeth and fired one more time. A blue hole appeared in Fletcher's forehead, and he fell, face down in the dirt. He twitched slightly and then stiffened and died.

Blue was conscious, but groaning with the pain of the wound. He relaxed, realizing that his opponent was dead. Darkness enveloped him and he heard no more for several hours.

On the street lay four men. Three of them were dead, and Blue lay unconscious.

A deep silence descended over Fall Creek, South Dakota, stretching into long, poignant moments.

21

Hoppy Jackson, Kemp and Charlie Shehan carried Blue's inert body to the Guthrie home. Placed on a cot in a room off the kitchen, he was attended by the widow, who was knowledgeable about gunshot wounds. In a few minutes he regained consciousness. He looked up into the tear-stained face of Ellen Turner and knew without a doubt that he loved her. With that peaceful thought he drifted off again until the elderly town doctor was brought in by Hoppy to attend to Blue.

He roused again when the doctor pulled down his pants, snipped away his undershirt and bared the wound. He gritted his teeth and groaned, and then as the doctor began pressing the wound and probing for any cloth shreds carried into it, he blacked out again.

At last the doctor completed his work

with the newly appointed Federal Marshal. He motioned for everyone to go into the living room.

'He is a strong young man. His good health and strength will be a deciding factor in his recovery.' He thought a moment and then continued, looking at Ellen and smiling, 'I should say that in about three weeks you can take him for a little ride in a buggy.'

Ellen blushed and then nodded. 'I'll see that he follows your orders, Doctor,' she said.

* * *

On the third week of Blue's recovery, Ellen had a buggy brought from the livery. It was warm, but nevertheless, she brought a light lap-robe and, fussing about him, made certain he was comfortable. Without further delay, she seized the reins and they drove out of town behind a trained buggy-mare.

'Ellen,' Blue said, 'the sheriff of the territory came while I was recovering.

He agreed that Hoppy and Kemp were well within their rights to protect me from ambush.' He was silent a moment.

'He told me,' Ellen said, 'that the N slash W ranch had been sold to an Eastern company. The money from the sale is in a Pierre bank, where I can draw on it for the cost of the buildings and house. That's where we are headed now, to look over the place, and see if I want to build back in the same spots, or in another place where we can build our home.'

He looked at her. 'We? I was just going to tell you I own a little horse-ranch in Blue River country in Arizona. I would sell it, bring a good stallion and some brood mares — '

'Yes,' she said.

'We could make a go of it — '

'Yes!'

He looked down into her eyes. 'Ellen, I want to marry you — '

'Yes!' She raised up. Holding his face in her palms, she kissed him sweetly and deeply, her lips clinging to his for a long moment.

They left the buggy and walked to a promontory overlooking her ranch. There they saw Hoppy and the other two men, along with three more, apparently nearby ranchers who had come as neighbors, helping clear away the burned timbers, removing the scars of the tragedy.

She put her head on his chest, her arms about his waist. 'I do have one question,' she said.

'What is that?'

'I don't really know your name. I'm certain there must be more than 'Blue'.'

He looked down at her and grinned wryly.

'Try Thomas Jackson Harrison,' he said, wincing. 'My pa was a jerk-leg politician and distant kin to William Henry Harrison. So I'm named after three presidents, and that makes a mouthful of a name!'

She pressed close to him. 'Where does 'Blue' come in?'

He grinned and hugged her. 'When I was a boy, I could run like a deer. I outran all my schoolmates, and some of their parents, in foot races. They started calling me Blue Streak, then shortened it to Blue. I've used that handle for years. It's easier to remember.'

She leaned back in his arms and smiled. 'That is a wonderful name. And I am proud to add my name to yours. However,' she paused.

'What?' he asked.

She hugged him close and murmured, 'Whatever your name I will always think of myself as Mrs Blue!'

They stood on the promontory, close together as one, letting the moments reach and linger, dreaming of the love that would hold them together for a lifetime.

Other titles in the
Linford Western Library:

MIDNIGHT LYNCHING

Terry Murphy

When Ruby Malone's husband is lynched by a sheriff's posse, Wells Fargo investigator Asa Harker goes after the beautiful widow expecting her to lead him to the vast sum of money stolen from his company. But Ruby has gone on the outlaw trail with the handsome, young Ben Whitman. Worse still, Harker finds he must deal with a crooked sheriff. Without help, it looks as if he will not only fail to recover the stolen money but also lose his life into the bargain.

BRAZOS STATION

Clayton Nash

Caleb Brett liked his job as deputy sheriff and being betrothed to the sheriff's daughter, Rose. What he didn't like was the thought of the sheriff moving in with them once they were married. But capturing the infamous outlaw Gil Bannerman offered a way out because there was plenty of reward money. Then came Brett's big mistake — he lost Bannerman and was framed. Now everything he treasured was lost. Did he have a chance in hell of fighting his way back?

SMOKING STAR

B. J. Holmes

In the one-horse town of Medicine Bluff two men were dead. Sheriff Jack Starr didn't need the badge on his chest to spur him into tracking the killer. He had his own reason for seeking justice, a reason no-one knew. It drove him to take a journey into the past where he was to discover something else that was to add even greater urgency to the situation — to stop Montana's rivers running red with blood.

THE WIND WAGON

Troy Howard

Sheriff Al Corning was as tough as they came and with his four seasoned deputies he kept the peace in Laramie — at least until the squatters came. To fend off starvation, the settlers took some cattle off the cowmen, including Jonas Lefler. A hard, unforgiving man, Lefler retaliated with lynchings. Things got worse when one of the squatters revealed he was a former Texas lawman — and no mean shooter. Could Sheriff Corning prevent further bloodshed?

CABEL

Paul K. McAfee

Josh Cabel returned home from the Civil War to find his family all murdered by rioting members of Quantrill's band. The hunt for the killers led Josh to Colorado City where, after months of searching, he finally settled down to work on a ranch nearby. He saved the life of an Indian, who led him to a cache of weapons waiting for Sitting Bull's attack on the Whites. His involvement threw Cabel into grave danger. When the final confrontation came, who had the fastest — and deadlier — draw?

BLACK RIVER

Adam Wright

John Dyer has come to the insignificant little town of Black River to destroy the last living reminder of his dark past. He has come to kill. Jack Hart is determined to stop him. Only he knows the terrible truth that has driven Dyer here, and he knows that only he can beat Dyer in a gunfight. Ex-lawman Brad Harris is after Dyer too — to avenge his family. The stage is set for madness, death and vengeance.